SIR WILLIAM WAAD

LIEUTENANT OF THE TOWER

THE GUNPOWDER PLOT

Fiona Bengtsen

Note for Librarians: A cataloguing record for this book is available from Library and Archives Canada at www.collectionscanada.ca/amicus/index-e.html
ISBN 1-4120-5541-5

Printed on paper with minimum 30% recycled fibre. Trafford's print shop runs on "green energy" from solar, wind and other environmentally-friendly power sources.

PUBLISHING™
Offices in Canada, USA, Ireland and UK
This book was published *on-demand* in cooperation with Trafford Publishing. On-demand publishing is a unique process and service of making a book available for retail sale to the public taking advantage of on-demand manufacturing and Internet marketing. On-demand publishing includes promotions, retail sales, manufacturing, order fulfilment, accounting and collecting royalties on behalf of the author.

Book sales for North America and international:
Trafford Publishing, 6E–2333 Government St.,
Victoria, BC v8t 4p4 CANADA
phone 250 383 6864 (toll-free 1 888 232 4444)
fax 250 383 6804; email to orders@trafford.com
Book sales in Europe:
Trafford Publishing (uk) Limited, 9 Park End Street, 2nd Floor
Oxford, UK oxi ihh UNITED KINGDOM
phone 44 (0)1865 722 113 (local rate 0845 230 9601)
facsimile 44 (0)1865 722 868; info.uk@trafford.com
Order online at:
trafford.com/05-0439

10 9 8 7 6 5 4

CONTENTS

Note: All dates are Old Style (year begins on Lady Day – March 25) unless otherwise stated.

ILLUSTRATIONS

DEDICATION

John Featherstone was Head of the English Department at Bishop's Stortford College, Hertfordshire. He died in July 1998, long before his time, after a protracted and courageous struggle against motor neurone disease. John's help was invaluable during the researching of the original material, of which this book is only a part.

We grasp the present only fleetingly, before both the moment, and we ourselves, become history.

With grateful thanks for the help and support of:

Frank and my family
Rosanne Kirkpatrick
Asa Loftner
Robin Wade
and
the encouragement of the Wade Family

Engraved by E.Bocquet.

SIR WILLIAM WAAD, KNT.

LIEUTENANT OF THE TOWER.

From a Picture, in the Possession of Frederick Holbrooke, Esqr.

of the Inner Temple.

Published May 1813, by White, Cochrane & Co.

PREFACE

Sir William Waad,
Lieutenant of the Tower of London

W HEN WILLIAM WAAD BECAME Lieutenant of the Tower of
London in August 1605, only three months before the Gunpowder
Plot, it was the culmination of a lifetime of service to the Crown.
On the eve of his appointment William had written to the Earl of
Salisbury* to thank him for his part in the promotion, and for the
long-standing support and patronage of the Cecil family. Obviously
pleased with his success, he expressed his 'tremendous happiness
that the Sovereign has seen fit to remember one now grown old
in the service of the State'.† At the age of fifty-nine he had finally
achieved his ambition. For the last twenty-two years he had been
a constant visitor to the Tower in his capacity as Secretary of the
Privy Council, where he had interrogated numerous prisoners on
behalf of the State, many of them under torture. Although some had
been released, or died in that hated place, many of those incarcerated owed their unfortunate position to his skill as an interrogator.
He had progressed from inquisitor to guardian. His father would
have been very proud of him, as between them they had served the
Crown and State for seventy years, from Henry VIII to James I.

---

* Robert Cecil, 1st Earl of Salisbury 1563-1612 (son of William Cecil).
† HMC XVII, Aug. 1605.

PRELUDE

Death in Dartford

O<small>N A HOT DAY</small> in July 1555, there was a bustle of activity at the gravel pit outside of Dartford. Great numbers of people were gathering to witness the burning of Christopher Waid, a protestant linen weaver. Laughing children darted through the forest of legs, as the fruiterers arrived with their horse-loads of cherries to assuage the thirst of the waiting multitude. At about 10 o'clock the sheriff arrived, in a great retinue, with his prisoner pinioned, but they passed by the gravel pit and went straight into town to make Christopher Waid ready for his execution. At the inn, he was stripped of his clothes, dressed in a long, clean white shirt brought by his wife, and led on foot to the pit. When they reached the site Christopher approached the pile of faggots[*] and embraced the stake, kissing it, before they set it against his back and placed it into a pitch barrel. A smith was called who brought an iron hoop and made him fast to the stake under his arms with two iron staples. Now fastened to the stake he lifted up his eyes and hands to heaven, repeating in a loud and cheerful voice the last verse of the 86th psalm – 'Shew some good token upon me, O Lord, that they which hate me may see it, and be ashamed: because thou Lord, hast helped me, and comforted me'.

Upon a hill close by there had been erected a pulpit where now entered a friar, book in hand. Waid became agitated on seeing the

---

[*] a bundle of sticks bound together as fuel.

Catholic friar and began to shout, exhorting the crowd not to listen to the whore of Babylon, but to embrace the gospel preached in the days of King Edward. 'Be quiet, Waid', interrupted the sheriff, 'and die quietly'. 'I am quiet', he replied, 'I thank God, Mr. Sheriff, and trust so to die'. All this time the friar looked on in amazement, then he withdrew without speaking a word and walked back into town.

Now the reeds were placed up against the martyr, and he gathered them up into his arms, and again addressed the people loudly. But the restless crowd would not listen and began to cast faggots at him, one striking him on the face. Then, as the fire was kindled, crackling and spitting as it caught, he cried unto God again and again, 'Lord Jesus, receive my soul', until his voice could be heard no more. The flames roared high into the air, so hot was the fire that the crowd stumbled back in fear of also being burnt. They watched in fascination as the flames licked at his corpse, creeping up his blackened arms raised above his head towards heaven, and up into his hands, until his fingers could swell no more with the heat, but burst one by one, releasing a black ooze that sizzled into the fire.

And so he died, 'with his hands still held together above his head, even when he was altogether roasted', said Richard Fletcher, the Kent cleric who witnessed the execution on that fateful day.[1]

Notes

1. Details from *Foxe's Book of Martyrs*.
Christopher Waid was the first of 61 Kentish Marian martyrs.
On East Hill, in Dartford, Kent, there is a monument to Christopher Waid and two other martyrs who were burnt at the stake in the town in 1555 during Queen Mary Tudor's reign.

SERO SED SERIO

Sir Robert Cecil, 1st Earl of Salisbury,
by John de Critz the Elder 1602
National Portrait Gallery

CHAPTER ONE

GENESIS – WILLIAM THE PERSECUTOR OF CATHOLICS

WILLIAM WAAD HATED CATHOLICS. Although we do not know if William witnessed the burning of Christopher Waid* at Dartford in 1555, it would certainly have been common knowledge in the extended Wade family that a Protestant cousin had been martyred by the Catholic Queen Mary. Family discussions about such a harrowing event would have had a profound effect upon a serious-minded, nine-year-old child like William and undoubtedly contributed to his hatred of Catholics.

William had been brought up and educated a Protestant under the patronage of the powerful Cecil family, because his father, Armigel, had served Sir William Cecil before becoming one of the first Clerks to the Privy Council† during the reign of King Henry VIII. Groomed by his father, William Waad followed in his footsteps to become Clerk to the Privy Council during the reigns of Queen Elizabeth I and King James I. For years he toiled ceaselessly, tracking down and questioning Catholic priests smuggled in from France and Spain, searching out Catholics involved in printing and distributing 'seditious' literature, and unravelling numerous plots to overthrow, or kill, the reigning monarchs and replace them with Catholic pretenders.

With his extensive background knowledge of previous plots and their perpetrators, who better than William Waad to work as

---

* Spellings of the name vary widely. William and his father both used the spelling Waad, but the name Wade is more commonly used by the family today.
† Privy Council – a group of high officials who gave private counsel to the ruling monarch.

1

Sir Robert Cecil's right-hand man in ferreting out the information about the Gunpowder Plot? As a known persecutor of Catholics, who better to assist Sir Robert Cecil in his quest to hang the Catholic cause once and for all, after it had so conveniently put its own head in the noose? In fact, who better than William Waad to become Lieutenant of the Tower of London a few months prior to the Gunpowder Plot?

There is no doubt that William Waad was collaborating with Sir Robert Cecil throughout the whole period of the plot, and that William Waad was installed at the Tower precisely because he could be relied upon to do Cecil's bidding without question. Without William Waad the outcome of this extra-ordinary plot may have been quite different. In fact Waad was so proud of his involvement in the investigation and resolution of the Gunpowder Plot that he erected an elaborate monument, commemorating the event, inside the Lieutenant's house at the Tower of London. The monument exists to this day.

William was born in 1546 during his father Armigel's six year tour of office as Clerk to the Council of Calais.[1] Armigel was a Yorkshireman, and an interesting character. He had been educated at Magdalen College, Oxford, before studying law in the Inns of Court in London. In April 1536, he set sail from Gravesend for the New World, with a 'party of gentlemen', in the 50 tonne 'Mignion'*.[2] Within two months he had reached New Foundland, and was back at St. Ives, Cornwall, by October 1536 after a memorable journey involving a brush with piracy and cannibalism.[3] Some have called him the 'English Columbus' as one of the first men to reach North America. He was 'a man who seemed to typify the spirit of the early Renaissance in England and to foreshadow the major achievements of the reign of Elizabeth I'.[4] Although Armigel was born into a Catholic country in 1511, the English state religion changed to Protestant during his twenties due to Henry VIII's reforms. Armigel's service to the state began when he served King Henry VIII in a minor way before being appointed to his first diplomatic post in France in November 1540. At that time Calais

---

* probably a carrack.

was a little piece of England on French soil. Here Armigel rubbed shoulders with kings and men-of-power, and learned the skills of diplomacy that were to assure his future career in the service of the State; knowledge which he passed on to his son.[5]

By September 1546 Armigel's tour of duty in France was over and he returned to England where Edward VI, the young son of Henry VIII, was now on the throne. He reported to the Chief Secretary of the Privy Council, Sir William Paget, who engaged him as Third Secretary. Six years later he was promoted to Chief Clerk and granted arms. Armigel and his son were to spend most of their lives working for Privy Councillors, directly or indirectly. The job of clerk was not only secretarial but involved ambassadorial duties as well as espionage, and it was now that the new Chief Clerk began to work with the complex spying system that was beginning to develop around the Crown. On April 14, 1552 Armigel paid his first visit to the Tower for a detailed interview with the Countess of Sussex who was accused of involvement in witchcraft. Little did he know then that fifty-three years later his own son would be Lieutenant of the Tower of London.[6]

Upon the accession of Catholic Queen Mary in 1553, William's father lost his post. Many Protestants left the country during this period, and although it would appear that Armigel did remain in England, he kept a low profile, taking seven year old William and the rest of his young family to live in various town and country properties,* where he engaged in writing pamphlets, one of which was ready for publication at the end of 1558 when Protestant fears subsided after Queen Mary's death from cancer.[7]

Armigel had raised his son very much in his own mould as a Servant of the State, and in preparation for this he sent twenty-one year old William to France in 1567. Throughout his life Armigel used his close contact with his friend Sir William Cecil in the upbringing of his son who had known Cecil since childhood. William Waad may even have been named after William Cecil.[8]

William Waad was twenty-two years old when his father died in 1568. He was one of seventeen children from Armigel's second

---

* like the ones in Soulbury, Buckinghamshire or Milton Bryant, Bedfordshire.

marriage, but at his mother's death there were only two sons and three daughters surviving.[9] Upon his father's death William inherited the lease on his father's house at Belsize in Hampstead, London which was to become one of his principal residences.[10]

After a brief stay in France, in 1571 at the age of twenty-five, Waad entered Gray's Inn to study law.[11] In his free time, he was able to work for Lord Burghley, as William Cecil now became, and he is known to have waited at table during the Queen Elizabeth's visit to her newly-promoted advisor in July 1572.[12]

His legal training now completed, Waad returned to France in May 1574. There are few personal details of his three year period in France but his return is announced in his diary, 'I came out of France from Tours to Greewiche Ano Dni. 1577'.[13] He was certainly living in Paris in the summer of 1576 and frequently supplied political information to Burghley, whose 'servant'* he is described as being. Burghley had attended St. John's College Cambridge at the, then not unusual, age of fourteen years, and it would be from this great seat of learning that both he and later his son Robert, would draw many willing participants to their service.[14]

Waad was in France during much of the 1570s when that country was in a terrible state as a result of the ongoing dispute between the Catholic Guise family and the Protestant Bourbons. William's father had been engaged in moving English troops across to France to assist the Huguenots† during the 1560s. The climax of all this pent-up hatred and bitterness between the two religious factions erupted on August 24, 1572 with the St. Bartholemew's Day Massacre in Paris, when French Huguenots were slaughtered by order of King Charles IX. When Waad arrived there the system of law and order had broken down and the currency system had virtually collapsed. There were considerable royal debts and public officials, who were unpaid, were pocketing public finances. In the countryside there were poor harvests with villagers sheltering in churches. Men like Waad were in danger of being captured by troops for a ransom,

---

* A 'servant' in this context means a person who supplies a service - as secretary, assistant or government agent, not a menial servant.
† Huguenots – French Protestants.

especially when they left the comparative safety of the town. At Blois, the parliament was dominated by the powerful Catholic Guise faction. Waad visited Blois in the autumn of 1576 with Sir Amyas Paulet, the English Ambassador at the French Court. Paulet left for France in September 1576 with his wife Margaret, and a retinue including fifteen-year-old Francis Bacon, a young man with whom William Waad would work closely later in his career. Francis is known to have accompanied Paulet to Blois, and must have been there at the same time as Waad.[15] The two probably knew each other well as both would have been regular visitors to William Cecil's home; Waad because of his long, close relationship with Burghley, through Armigel, and Francis Bacon because his mother, Ann Cook, was the sister of Mildred who was married to Burghley. In 1576 William Waad was aged thirty and Francis Bacon half his age, but although both these young men were learning the art of diplomacy with Paulet, there was considerable difference in their status because Bacon was Burghley's nephew.

Paulet was delighted with Waad's progress and potential as an intelligence-gatherer and diplomat, and recommended him to Burghley in his letters.[16] Waad learnt, through Paulet's example, that even minor matters should not be ignored as these accumulated facts often lead to important conclusions. This experience in the collection and assessment of detail was to be a vital factor in William Waad's success as an interrogator.

After his three years in France, Waad became a roving intelligence gatherer as he moved around Europe forwarding reports to Burghley and Paulet. When he was in Venice in April 1579, he sent the Lord Treasurer Burghley fifty of the rarest seeds and plants in Italy.[17] As Burghley was a keen gardener who admired the new and fashionable Italianate garden, Waad knew that such gifts would be very acceptable to him. It would also do no harm to his prospects of promotion. In May 1579, William was in Florence and during that summer he visited Portugal and Spain.[18] The Venetian Ambassador in Madrid reported on the activities of the English Ambassador – thought to be William – who had arrived at Lisbon thoroughly seasick and fatigued.[19] He arrived in Madrid at an unfortunate time when news had just been received that English ships had attacked a Spanish fleet on its return from India, and captured a vessel carrying more than 600,000 crowns. Because Waad was known to be a committed Protestant and to hate Catholics, he was considered a 'very great heretic'. He was received by the Spanish king only very briefly and dismissed in great haste. By August 1579 he was ready to return to England, by land.[20] His journey back home took him through Strasburg[21] from where he reported on the movements of the leader of the mercenary army, Duke John Casimir, who seemed to be levying troops for the King of Spain when Queen Elizabeth was paying him to assist the Huguenots and the Dutch.[*] From there Waad traveled to Paris where he joined Sir Henry Brooke (Lord Cobham), who had succeeded Sir Amias Paulet as resident ambassador there.[22] Brooke had a 'very good opinion of Mr. Wade'.[23] He seems to have genuinely liked William as well as being impressed by his potential. So much so, that when Waad left Paris for England on June 9, 1580 he carried with him a letter from Brooke to Walsingham[†] suggesting that, 'Mr. Wade be presented to her majesty with good recommendations [that] he may be accepted as her sworn servant', because he had already shown the ability to serve her on that 'side of the sea'.[24]

William was back in England by 1581 when he became Francis Walsingham's secretary. Another product of Cambridge University, like the Cecils, Walsingham had used his contacts at the university to recruit suitable young men into his newly-formed secret service after he became Queen Elizabeth's Secretary of State, in 1573.[25] During his travels over the past few years William Waad too had been learning these special arts, and in time he would put them to great use. There were no newspapers or other methods of receiving information from abroad at that time, so every scrap of information, no matter how insignificant, was eagerly devoured by the authorities in England. There were agents, observers and an army of other foreign correspondents who acted as the eyes and ears of the government abroad. Not all were spies in the accepted sense of the

[*] Elizabeth I, a Protestant Queen, was supporting the Protestant Huguenots in France, as well as the Protestants in the Netherlands, against the occupying Spanish.
[†] Sir Francis Walsingham, Secretary of State.

word, but there was considerable cross-over between the spy and the intelligencer. Waad was an 'intelligencer', the equivalent perhaps of a media journalist today, and had been instructed to report on everything when sending reports to Walsingham from the Continent, using the 'express system'* for vital news. He worked closely with Thomas Phelippes, Walsingham's assistant who became a skilled code-breaker. In Elizabethan England, because all correspondence had to be transported either physically or orally this left enormous scope for interception by outsiders, so it was essential that Waad should learn to use the ciphers so important to the safe transmission of letters. Symbols and numbers were often used to represent individuals: in 1597, Jesuits were '90', the Lord Treasurer '80' and Waad himself number '70'.[26] In 1595, Waad had a different cipher, he was then a symbol shown as $\times$ and)(. Through Arthur Gregory, Phelippes' aide, William must also have learned the art of forcing the seal of a letter so skilfully that it was impossible to see the tamper;[27] a trick he was to use to great effect later in his career. During his travels, Waad had also sent saplings to Walsingham as he had previously done to Burghley,[28] and Walsingham was almost certainly instrumental in enabling Waad to become one of the clerks to the Privy Council in 1583.

There appear to have been about four clerkships of the Privy Council at any one time, with clerks working on a rota basis. When Waad joined, Thomas Wilkes had been a clerk since 1576, but suffered a spell out of favour in 1587 and did not resume the position until 1589. Robert Beale, another of Waad's contemporaries became clerk in July 1572, Beale, like William Waad, had also worked for Walsingham. Both are described as case-officers, confidential messengers and private secretaries during that time.[29] The clerks operated independently but did occasionally work together. Waad and Beale are both recorded as examining a suspected Catholic malcontent, Richard Brookman, at the Tower in 1590.[30] Wilkes and Waad examined and tortured a Frenchman in Bridewell in 1595/6 who was found to be carrying suspicious papers.[31] Anthony Ashley was

---

* 'Express system' - A fast rider on horseback who used recognized staging
  posts to switch to fresh horses.

another clerk with whom Waad sometimes worked, but although Ashley became clerk in 1587 he was suspended from his post in 1591 and not reinstated until 1603, so his clerkship did not coincide with much of Waad's term of office. Thomas Smith's entry into service as a clerk was secured in 1595 by Robert Devereux, 2nd Earl of Esssex, for whom Smith worked as chief secretary. Thomas Edmondes was another of Waad's colleagues; a Privy Council clerk who had also worked for Walsingham.* All the Privy Council clerks complained that the clerkship was not a very lucrative position. If Queen Elizabeth had been thought parsimonious, then James's reign was no more rewarding for government officers. Waad moaned 'that the council chamber yields little profit. The oldest officers in Court retire themselves and those more young with money are suffered to purchase preferment'.[32] However, the job did open up some interesting possibilities for the more diligent among them. In fact, several of these clerks would be rewarded for their services in 1603.

Now, as an expert linguist in French, Italian and Latin, William was sent by the Privy Council on missions abroad, and in April 1583 he departed on a four month tour of major European capitals for a variety of diplomatic purposes. This period of nine years of almost continual travel around Europe concluded a phase of his training. The young spy and informer had become a diplomat and he was now ready to face more challenging situations.

Waad's first diplomatic mission for Queen Elizabeth I was the unenviable task of explaining to the Spanish king why Mendoza, their ambassador in London, had been expelled in January 1584, for plotting against Elizabeth. When Waad arrived in Madrid in March, Philip II refused to see him or even listen to his arguments. Waad persisted, only to be shown the door by an irate king. 'In dark and doubtful terms', he was told that, 'he was favourably dealt with and might have looked for worse entertainment'.[33] Upon Waad's safe return to England on April 12, 1584, diplomatic relations between England and Spain ceased and the danger of a Spanish invasion increased. Nor was his next task any easier, for this time he attempted the impossible, a reconciliation between Mary Queen of Scots and

*Wilkes (1545-1598); Beale (1541-1601); Ashley (1551/2-1628); Smith (1556-1609); Edmundes (d.1639). DNB on-line.

Queen Elizabeth I. In this mission he again failed miserably, although he certainly succeeded in enraging Mary when he had the audacity to point out that her treatment by Elizabeth was 'as one of the rarest examples of singular mercy and good inclination that was ever heard of'.[34] Nevertheless, his doggedness and sheer persistence must have impressed those in authority because on October 7, 1584 he was promoted to the life-time office of Clerk of the Privy Council through the recommendation of Lord Burghley.

In these character-building years of diplomatic activity Waad crossed the Channel to Paris several times. On the next occasion he tried to obtain the extradition of Thomas Morgan, a Welsh Catholic working for Mary Queen of Scots, for his part in the Parry Plot.[35] This time Waad was at least partially successful as he persuaded the French King, Henry III, to keep Morgan restrained in the Bastille, although Morgan still managed to help to organize the next plot against Queen Elizabeth from his prison cell. Despite the French King's begrudging co-operation there were other factions at work in France, and the Catholic Guise family was not going to surrender easily one of their staunch supporters like Morgan. So it was that Waad and his four attendants were ambushed by Duke d'Aumale's henchmen near Abbeville in Picardy and punished with a severe beating. Waad had been lucky to escape unharmed in his dealings with the Spanish king and now he was lucky to escape with his life. He returned to England in early April 1585, 'much discontented'.[36]

Battles Hall, Manuden

About a year after his return to England, William married Ann Waller in London in 1586.[37] Ann was the daughter of Owen Waller, a member of the Fishmongers' Company of London, who lived at Parham, Suffolk and Wood Street, London. This fifteen-year-old girl married William Waad when he had just turned forty, and there appears to have been a child from the marriage.[38] Sadly, Ann lived only three years more, before she died in childbirth.[39] Among the properties William inherited through Ann was Battles Hall estate and manor house in Manuden, Essex, near Bishop's Stortford, to which he later retired,[40] and a house in Wood Street beside the Counter Prison, in the City of London, which he found extremely useful when required to spend many hours at the gaol questioning prisoners. After his marriage, Waad spent some time at his estate in Manuden which was less then a mile from the home of Thomas Crowley, one of the most obstinate and unyielding 'popish' recusants in the county. For years Crowley, of Manuden Hall, suffered not only fines but years of imprisonment for his faith. In the Returns of Recusants[*] for the Diocese of London for 1577, the Bishop of

---

[*]A list of Catholics liable to fines or punishment for non-attendance at Protestant church services.

London presented Crowley to the Quarter Sessions for non-attendance at church for more than twenty years. In 1581 he was still in 'a prison called the White Lion Southwark'. In 1587 he was fined £80, committed for 'Papistrie' and sent to Colchester Gaol.[41] Many devout Catholics absented themselves from the Protestant church during this time as a matter of principle, but would never have dreamed of being traitors to their country or their queen. In fact when he died, despite his harsh treatment by the community, Crowley bequeathed money to the poor of all the local villages including the handsome sum of five pounds to the Parish of Manuden. He also requested burial in the chancel of the local church, but he seems to have been denied this last wish.

In the same year that he married, William Waad helped to provide the fatal evidence that sent the Scottish Queen to the scaffold for her part in the Babington Plot.[42] This must have been a major coup for a man who hated Catholics. The plan to entrap Mary Queen of Scots involved intercepting Mary's letters, which were being smuggled in and out Chartley House, in Staffordshire, where the Queen of Scots was being held under house arrest for conspiring against Queen Elizabeth. The letters were transported in barrels of beer, but a double-agent was passing Mary's letters first to Walsingham and then to Phelippes who deciphered and copied them before returning them to be replaced in the barrels. This intercepted correspondence resulted in the arrest of Anthony Babington and his co-conspirators, but did not provide sufficient evidence against Mary's involvement, so Waad was called in to search her rooms at Chartley. While Mary was lured away from the house to hunt stag on a nearby estate, William Waad and Sir Amyas Paulet ransacked her apartments where they found a huge haul of correspondence, plus a valuable collection of sixty secret ciphers buried in the garden. The Council now had their first positive evidence of Mary's links with Catholic conspirators. She was tried by a jury of noblemen and found guilty of treason. A week later, on February 8, 1587 her head was severed from her body at Fotheringay Castle in Northamptonshire. The Scottish Queen died with dignity, but when the executioner lifted up her head it is said that her auburn wig slipped off showing her grey hair beneath it. Those present were convinced that her lips continued to move in prayer. Queen Elizabeth was horrified at what she had done and the speed at which the execution was administered. The remorse she suffered lasted long after the event.

Despite the death of Mary, and the failure of the Spanish attack upon England in 1588,[43] the threat from Catholics was considered to be even more serious than before. One of William Waad's tasks during this period was to track down and question 'papists'. Philip Howard, the Earl of Arundel, had been imprisoned in 1586 for being a Romanist,* fleeing the country without the Queen's permission, intriguing with priests and claiming the title of Duke of Norfolk. Waad was requested to gather evidence against him for his trial on a charge of high treason, in April 1589, which he did by persuading the priest William Bennet to testify that the Earl had prayed for the success of the Spanish Armada. At his trial the Earl's lofty bearing and magnificent attire did nothing to help his cause and he was found guilty. He was to remain a prisoner in the Tower for the rest of his life.[44] Waad's fearsome reputation as an interrogator and hunter of dangerous or disaffected Catholics is captured in a letter from the Earl of Derby to the Council, advising that the hunt for priests in Cheshire and Lancashire was not going well. Apparently, when the Catholics heard that William Waad had been sent into their area they became extremely cautious, and had all gone to ground.[45]

As William Waad now expected to spend more time in England he decided to remarry, some nine years after the death of his first wife. By this time he was fifty-two years old. The evidence for this appears in a letter from his co-clerk on the Privy Council, Sir Anthony Ashley. He wrote, 'My fellow Wade is married', then in a punning piece of Latin adds *dominus ex audivit me et erixit cornua salutes mei'* (the Lord has listened to me and raised up the horn of my salvation).[46] This amusing note could well refer to a rhinoceros horn, known as an aphrodisiac in its powdered form, which is still in the possession of the Wade family, and is believed to have been given to William in 1581, following his visit to Portugal as ambassador for Queen Elizabeth.[47]

---

*Romanist – member or supporter of the Roman Catholic Church.

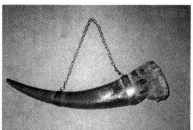

Sir. Wm. Waad's crest

The Wade Rhinoceros Horn

William's second marriage was to Anne, the daughter of the late Humphrey Browne, his father's old friend, who had been a Justice of the Common Pleas and had served with Armigel Waad as a JP for Midddlesex. Anne was born c.1563/4, making her about seventeen years younger than William. She probably knew him all her life due to their fathers' close personal relationship. As a posthumous child Anne had been made a Ward of Court which meant she inherited very little from her father's will, so she would no doubt have considered William a good catch.[48] The historian Richard Symonds, who visited Manuden Church in September 1639, where William had spent his latter years, wrote: 'Sir William Waad had fifteen children by his second lady, to whome he sware marriage if she would swear that ye child she then went withal, was of his begetting, and he married her… None of all these fifteen but had some imperfection. Those that were strait and handsome were dumb or deaf, those of them that could speake were lame or crooked'.[49] Yet despite Anne's assurance of her fidelity, Sir William does not appear to have married her until 1599, two years after the birth of daughter Abigail on January 21, 1597.[50]

Portrait of a Lady, said to be Lady Anne Waad
Oil on canvas
Marcus Gheeraerts the Younger (1561-1635)
Courtesy of Sotheby's

After a few more years of difficult missions abroad, William Waad had a change of career as he was now required to investigate the numerous plots against the Queen.[51] For this occupation his years of training in the black arts of espionage, plus his experience in the field, and the determination and persistence inherent in his character, made him admirably suited. He also found that not only was he an excellent interrogator, able to extract information from unwilling subjects, but he actually enjoyed the job, indeed he excelled in this field. This fact was not lost on Robert Cecil who now increasingly used his services. Even before the death of Sir William Cecil in 1598, William Waad had begun working with his son Sir Robert Cecil, so that by the time Queen Elizabeth died in 1603, Waad already knew who would succeed her and was looking forward to meeting his new monarch.

Notes

1 Official title: 'Clerk to the Council in the Town and Marches of Calais'.
2 Foster, Alumni Oxoniensis; Fuller, p.202.
3 Haklyt Vol.III, pp120-131.
4 Winchester, p.40.
5 Park, p.138.
6 CSP Edward VI, May 30, 1552.
7 Pamphlet: 'Distresses of the Commonwealth with ye meanes to remedy them' Archaeologia 13, 169: Birch, f.343.
8 Sir William Cecil (1520-1598) Chief Secretary of State to Eliz. I. Created Lord Burghley 1571, Lord High Treasurer of England 1572. DNB p.406 onward.
9 William; Thomas who was to become an important lawyer, and the three daughters, Joyce, Ann, and Margaret. Margaret married Robert Jones, Clerk of the Privy Seal.
10 PC Lyon 6.
11 Register of Admission to Gray's Inn, 1521-1889 p.42.
12 HMC Cecil Vol. 5, 140 p.37.
13 Erobus Calendar Rawlinson Manuscripts.
14 DNB, p.406.
15 du Maurier ,*The Golden Lads*, p.39/40.
16 Amyas Paulet Letter Books p.288 onward.
17 CSP Domestic, Elizabeth. Mar. 25, 1579, p. 12.
18 HMC II, May 19, 1579.
19 CSP Venetian, Aug. 12, 1579 from Madrid.
20 HMC II, Aug. 21, 1579.
21 CSP Foreign, Elizabeth, Feb. 16, 1580, and HMC II, Mar. 7, 1579-80, p.315.
22 DNB on-line version, Henry Brooke.
23 CSP Foreign, Elizabeth, June 8, 1580.
24 ibid June 9, 1580, p.301.
25 Queen Elizabeth invested regular sums of public money which made this an official organization and thus the 'first' official secret service in England.
26 CSP Ireland 1601-3 Addenda, Comyn to Earl of Essex 1597.
27 Nicholl, pp. 127,129.
28 CSP Domestic, Elizabeth, 1581-90 March 25, 1581.
29 Nicholl, p.130.
30 APC 1590.

31 ibid Jan. 1595/6.
32 Papers of Ralph Winwood, Vol. II, p.4.
33 CSP Venetian, p.248.
34 Froude Vol 12, p.626.
35 The Parry Plot. – Doctor William Parry, MP, planned to place Mary Queen of Scots on throne of England after he had murdered Elizabeth as she was walking in St. James's Park.
36 Erobus Calendar.
37 London Marriage Licenses, p.145.
38 Probably Armygild who was registered at Grays Inn in 1618. It is not known if this child survived and entered Grays Inn, but a second child called Armigel was born in c.1603 and died aged 7 in 1611. It was unusual to have two children living in the same family with the almost identical names. Nothing is known either, of how this child was cared for after the mother's death.
39 Ann was buried at St. Alban's Church, Wood Street, London. The tower from a much later church is all that survives. This is now a private dwelling. Her memorial in St. Alban's Church is recorded in Stowe's Survey of London as, 'A fair marble monument in oval'. p.78.
40 William rebuilt Battles Hall on a new site some time after he married Ann Waller.
41 Returns of Recusants: Diocese of London 1577 & Essex Quarter Sessions 1581-2.
42 Froude Vol. 12, p.160; Babington Plot – Francis Walsingham's secret service intercepted and read all letters passing between the captive Mary, Queen of Scots, and Anthony Babington and his Catholic conspirators. The plot was to assassinate Queen Elizabeth and place Mary on the throne.
43 The Spanish Armada was destroyed by the English fleet.
44 Atttainder of Philip Howard, Earl of Arundel 1589 BL MSS.
45 CSP Domestic Eliz. Derby to Council Nov. 1592, p.268.
46 CSP Domestic Eliz. Sir Anthony Ashley to Lord Cobham, Jan. 17, 1597/8.
47 DNB on-line; a rhinoceros is employed as a crest in Waad's coat-of-arms.
48 Wardship – the under-age child of a major landowner became a piece of property when a parent died. Wardships were sold, and the owner ran the child's estates until he/she came of age.
49 Visitation of Manuden, R. Symonds.
50 Mort Commons, p. 324. There is only evidence of these disabilities in one child named in William's Will who is provided for her 'infirmity'.
51 Dr. Lopez Plot to poison Queen Eliz. in 1594 – one of many such plots.
52 Sir Robert Cecil, knighted 1591 (DNB on-line).

King James VI of Scotland and James I of England
after John De Critz the Elder – National Portrait Gallery

CHAPTER TWO

THE ARRIVAL OF KING JAMES I

LONG BEFORE KING JAMES'S carriage swept into the driveway of Sir Robert Cecil's principal residence of Theobalds, in Hertfordshire, on that fine spring day of May 3, 1603, William Waad had already arrived.

Ever since Sir Robert Carey's frantic ride north, on March 24, 1603, to deliver the news of Queen Elizabeth's death to King James VI of Scotland, the whole country had been on the move, with supporters and sycophants anxious to gain favour with the newly-proclaimed King James I of England. James, who was eager to claim his new crown in London, set off on the journey south on April 5, stopping at various towns and cities on the way to visit the great and the good. At each location he conferred knighthoods by the score which would naturally boost his support in the country. On the morning of April 18, in York, where the retinue had stopped overnight, Mr. Secretary, Sir Robert Cecil came to meet his new sovereign, though they had been secretly corresponding for some time before Queen Elizabeth's death.[1] This was a momentous meeting between two men with strong minds trapped inside defective bodies, who would need to learn to work together. James made light of their meeting, quipping to Cecil that, 'though you are but a little man we will shortly load your shoulders with business'.[2] Cecil, knelt dutifully, but he would come to dislike his monarch's nickname for him of 'my little beagle'.[3] After travelling south with James's entourage for six days, Cecil managed to slip away back to London where he arrived on April 25, not only to continue his business but to make arrangements for the King's entertainment at 'Theobalds', Sir Robert's home in Hertfordshire. On Cecil's orders this splendid red brick, renaissance palace with its courts, fountains and elaborate gardens had been scrubbed and polished until it was fit to receive its royal visitor and his court.[4]

When the King's carriage stopped outside Theobalds on May 3, 1603, William Waad, Clerk of the Privy Council, was on hand to serve his new monarch. With his beard neatly clipped, and dressed in his best, fur-trimmed gown, William's sharp eyes took in every detail, as he had been trained to do. The King emerged nursing a badly bruised arm which he had received when he fell from his horse near Burghley-by-Stamford where Robert Cecil's elder half brother[*] had entertained the king a few days earlier.[5] This had curtailed James's horse-riding activities temporarily much to his displeasure, for he enjoyed the hunt. William observed that the king was short in stature, with a strange gait due to his twisted foot, but he exuded a royal presence. This was no inexperienced prince, but the son of Mary Queen of Scots and Lord Darnley. James had already been King of Scotland for thirty-six years since the abdication of his mother in 1567, when he was only one year old. He was dressed in heavily padded breeches and doublet, his body armour against would-be assassins. This paranoia was a legacy of the king's turbulent youth in Scotland, when he had witnessed murder and mayhem.

At the age of five he had seen his dying grandfather, the Earl of Lennox, being carried into Stirling Castle after Lennox was shot in the back during an attempted coup by supporters of James's own mother. Seven years later, the terrified twelve-year-old witnessed more bloodshed at Stirling Castle during another coup, when several men were killed. Then, in August 1582 when he was sixteen, he was kidnapped by the Ruthven Lords,[†] who held him captive for ten months until this enterprising youth managed to escape. From then on, James had directed his own destiny, so that this motherless and lonely but bright little boy, who had grown up without siblings or any suggestion of a loving environment, developed into an intelligent, confident ruler.

James's final brush with violence in Scotland occurred on

---

[*] Thomas Cecil, now 2nd Lord Burghley after the death of his father.
[†] The Earls of Gowrie.

August 5, 1600, near Falkland, during the so-called Gowrie Conspiracy, when the King was lured from a hunt by the Master of Ruthven (the grandson of those who had kidnapped him as a child), to Lord Gowrie's house in Perth. There he found himself trapped in the turret facing an armed and armoured man. What happened next is still disputed, but following a struggle the king's page, James Ramsay, came to his aid and stabbed the assailant to death. It never emerged why the King exhibited such strange conduct as to visit the home of a nobleman hostile to him, but there are suggestions that the act was a result of the King's homosexual advances to the handsome young Ruthven, which were rejected. Whatever the reason, King James forever considered August 5 as a day of thankful remembrance for his miraculous escape from death, a day which was to be superceded by another fifth day of the month in 1605.[6]

When the King stepped down from his carriage outside Theobalds many members of Robert Cecil's estate staff were lined up to pay their respects to him. As he approached they flung their hats into the air joyfully and clapped as he entered the building. Most of Elizabeth's Privy Council were there to meet him, all anxious to make a good impression on their new monarch. Sir Thomas Egerton was one of these.[7] James would re-appoint him as Lord Keeper briefly, but Egerton would relinquish this position in July 1603 when he became Lord Chancellor. Baron Ellesmere, as he then became, would find his path converge several times with that of William Waad during the next fourteen years when he presided over the chancery and Star Chamber. Ellesmere would conduct a number of important state trials, notably that of Sir Walter Ralegh in 1603, the gunpowder plotters in 1605, and Robert Carr, the Earl of Somerset and his wife Frances' trial in 1616,[8] all cases which would closely involve William Waad. The Earl of Northumberland, Sir Henry Percy, had also arranged to meet the king. This high-ranking lord had been corresponding with the king prior to his succession, but he was unaware that Cecil also knew about his letters. Northumberland's purpose now was to present a petition on behalf of Catholics, requesting greater religious tolerance.[9] This was an act he would later come to rue as it established him, in the king's eyes, as the unofficial head of the Catholic Church, a position that was destined to land him in untold trouble in the future. He too would cross the path of William Waad.

The next day May 4, 1603, the King sat in Council at Theobalds with his chief lords for the swearing-in ceremony of William Waad, Thomas Smith and Thomas Edmunds who took the oath of Clerks of His Highnesses Privy Council, posts they had held in the previous reign. In fact, William had already served the Privy Council for twenty years under Elizabeth following his apprenticeship in France to learn the crafts of diplomacy and espionage. This knowledge he immediately employed when he returned to England to work for Sir Francis Walsingham, the controller of England's first Secret Service, which had been master-minded by William Cecil in 1570. When Walsingham died in 1590, William Cecil's son, Robert Cecil, became Secretary of State and inherited this intelligence network from him. Now William Waad reported to Robert who was seventeen years his junior. Not only had Waad worked for both William and Robert Cecil, but he had grown up under the patronage of the family, and had known Robert from childhood.

Although James stayed on a further three days at Theobalds, William Waad took his leave shortly after the ceremony and rode back to his house at Belsize to check on his family. There was plague in London, and as Clerk to the Council there was much work to do issuing orders throughout the country to limit the effects of the disease. William was alarmed because panic-stricken Londoners were escaping to the heights of Hampstead, near his home, and bringing 'bedding and stuff with them'. Many were dying under the hedges and in fields or even entering 'men's yards and outhouses if they be open and dye ther'.[10]

The most important event of 1603 which would bring people together in the City of London was the arrival of King James. On May 11 James entered the Tower of London where he toured the armoury, visited the church and viewed the multifarious facilities of this ancient castle. Three days later he departed for Greenwich, and although he kept well away from the main streets he was still mobbed by crowds wherever he went. All were curious to see their new monarch despite the risk of contagion in the plague-ridden city. Danger from the Plague meant that James's coronation had to be postponed until July 25, 1603 and his arrival ceremony switched was to a boat journey on the Thames, to distance him for any crowds that might gather. A rare proclamation had to be issued commanding gentlemen to depart the Court and City and not to return until the Coronation.

Sixteen days after James left Theobalds, William Waad was knighted at the Palace of Greenwich along with two other Clerks of the Privy Council.[11]

Notes

1 Correspondence of King James VI with Robert Cecil & Others, p.7 passim.
2 HMC Salisbury, XIV, p.162.
3 Akrigg, letter 105, p.277.
4 Hatfield MSS, April 4, 1603, p.49, Burghley to Robert Cecil; Bruce, p.7; King James so loved the house that he swapped it with Robert Cecil for Hatfield House. James died at Theobalds on Mar. 27, 1625. Note: Theobalds original house was demolished in 1641.
5 Nichols, *Progresses of James I,* Vol. 1, p.96.
6 Bryan Bevan, *King James VI of Scotland & I of England*, pp.61/2.
7 Nichols, p.107.
8 DNB on-line version, Thomas Egerton.
9 Nichols, pp.138-9.
10 Barratt, letter: Waad to Cecil, p.64.
11 Nichols, p.55 ; Waad, Edmundes and Smith were knighted on May 20, 1603.

CHAPTER THREE

THE PRECURSORS

The Essex Rebellion and Plots Bye and Main

QUEEN ELIZABETH'S LIFE CAME to an end in March 1603, some six months before her seventieth birthday. Throughout her long reign there had been innumerable plots and threats to her life, some only trifling, others more serious, which continued even into her old age, like the Essex Plot of 1601. William Waad had been one of the principal investigators into almost all of these plots, including the Essex Rebellion and plots Bye and Main, which meant that he knew the plotters and their backgrounds intimately. This knowledge was to become a valuable tool in examining the perpetrators of the Gunpowder Treason.

The Essex Rebellion of 1601 involved Robert Devereux, 2nd Earl of Essex, the rising star of Elizabeth's government, who was eclipsed by the shadow of Ireland.* This tall, pale-skinned, handsome man with a wispy, red beard became one of the Queen's favourites. But he was inexperienced at court, and completely lacked a sense of proportion which meant that when he became troublesome in April 1599, Elizabeth dispatched him to Ireland to command her army. William Shakespeare's friend, Henry Wriothesley, the Earl of Southampton, accompanied him, despite the Queen's orders to the contrary, along with Essex's stepfather Sir Christopher Blount, (a convert to Catholicism). Essex's orders were to proceed against the rebel Irishman, Hugh O'Neill,† 'The Arch Traitor Tyrone', but

---

* DNB on-line, Devereux (1565-1601).
† Earl of Tyrone.

instead he negotiated with Tyrone. Elizabeth was furious. To try to make amends, the impulsive Essex rushed back to England, bursting into the Queen's chamber at Nonsuch Palace in Surrey, without permission and before she was fully dressed. This was the final straw. He was arrested and finally charged in June 1600. Deprived of his offices and confined to Essex House in the Strand, he felt humiliated and began to conspire against the state. Despite Essex's upbringing as a Ward of Court in the household of William Cecil, both at Theobalds and Cecil House in the Strand, where he mixed with Cecil's sharp-minded son, Robert Cecil, there had been no love lost between them.[1] Essex believed Elizabeth was being corrupted by her inner circle of councillors which included Robert Cecil, and vowed to free her of these men. When four Privy Councillors became aware of the partially hatched plot in February 1601, they visited him at Essex House only to be confronted by his supporters and locked in a room. Meanwhile, Essex tried to implement his badly conceived rebellion. Full details of the debacle emerged later under questioning by Dr. Julius Caesar and William Waad. The Earl and his supporters had marched along the Strand to St. Paul's, then into Gracechurch Street where they turned back to Ludgate. By this time Lord Burghley, with three hundred citizens, was approaching. When the opposing parties met at Cheapside, a lively fight broke out with shots fired and rapiers drawn. One man was killed and several injured. When the action failed Essex returned by boat to his house, surrendered, and was taken to the Tower.[2]

William Waad, with several others, was asked to examine those apprehended in connection with the Essex plot and to meet together to decide on their strategy. After numerous examinations at the Court of Whitehall by Lord Keeper Egerton, Secretary Cecil and William Waad, they were supremely confident in informing Attorney General Coke and Francis Bacon that 'although by the former examinations the treasons of the Earl were sufficiently discovered, yet by the pains taken this day their rebellious purposes are so layed open, that all the world may be fully satisfied'. Essex was put to death on February 25, 1601, on a specially erected scaffold in the Tower of London, but William was kept busy for months questioning his supporters, many of whom would also be executed.[3]

Among those rounded up and held at various prisons in London were: Robert Catesby, who was held at the Wood Street Counter;* Ambrose Rookwood, Thomas Winter, Francis Tresham at Newgate Prison; and Mr. Parker (Lord Monteagle) at the Tower. John Grant, John Wright and Christopher Wright at the White Lyon; and Sir Edward Lyttleton at the Fleet.[4] All these people were eventually released, some after payment of huge fines. Relieved to have escaped with their lives, the men retired to their homes in the Midlands to recuperate from their ordeal, but history would call them again very soon.

Sir William Waad was also instrumental in examining new plots being hatched in the first few years of James' reign, the earliest of which are generally referred to as the Bye and Main Plots. Although there was some overlap in the people involved, the Bye Plot was an attempt by Catholics to seize the King in order to force him to be more favourable towards Catholics, whereas in the Main Plot the plan was to kill the King and his family, to encourage a Spanish army to land at Milford Haven, and to place Lady Arabella Stuart on the throne.[†]

Sir Robert Cecil's hair was turning grey at forty years old when Queen Elizabeth died in March 1603, but he still retained his brilliant mind and his vigour. He had learned to live with the disability of a misshapen back, at a time in history where such physical deformities were considered a mark of the devil. His preparation for the transition between Elizabethan and Stuart rule was flawless, even ensuring that dissident factions like Robert Catesby were locked up to prevent trouble. And although trouble was expected, it was soon obvious that the people were happy with their new sovereign. James was a family man, unlike their previous virgin Queen, and he brought with him a wife and three young children to his new country, much to the delight of the populace.[5]

The succession of James VI of Scotland to the throne of England as James I had given the Catholic community in England new hope. For years under Elizabeth, they had suffered hefty fines

*Waad lived next door to the Wood Street Counter, where he interrogated many prisoners.
†Arabella Stuart was the cousin of King James I.

25

and even imprisonment for their decision to become recusants by refusing to worship in Protestant churches. Long before his journey south, James had given courtiers and priests alike the distinct impression that he intended to pursue a more liberal attitude towards Catholics when he became King of England, and indeed his early letters to Robert Cecil do convey suggestions of this attitude.[6] It was also known that the king was keen to negotiate a peace treaty with Spain. Encouraging factors like the conversion of James's wife, Anne of Denmark, to Catholicism, the restoration of Lords Arundel, Westmorland and Paget, all known to favour the Roman Catholic religion, and the knighthoods given to numerous, well-known recusants were good signs, but, after less than a year in the south, James became convinced of the impracticality of this idea. As a shrewd Scotsman he soon realised that the revenue received from recusants was a welcome addition to the treasury, and he began to clamp down again on this community whose numbers were reported to be growing in the north, since 'the penalties had not been enforced so rigorously of late'. They were also 'becoming, very insolent... and some go up and down to get a petition for toleration of religion'.[7] When the Catholic community eventually realised that James was not to be their saviour, stirrings of discontent began to ripple through certain layers of society.

The chief participants in the Bye Plot of 1603 were the Catholic priests William Watson and Francis Clarke, Lord Grey, Sir Griffin Markham, Lord Henry Cobham's brother George Brooke and Anthony Copley. When questioned, some of them also implicated Sir Walter Ralegh. Copley named John Scudamore as an accessory to the conspiracy. William Waad questioned John's father, Thomas Scudamore, who gave little support to his son, admitting that he was capable of fraudulent dealings and malicious behaviour which he blamed on his wife, Amy. Thomas wanted the release of his son, and in return offered to find and detain the priest Watson. Copley too, was anxious to distance himself from the others. He offered information about some of the Jesuit suspects and their plots. Waad eventually managed to extract a confession from the Markham brothers, but only after Sir Griffin had given permission to his brothers, Charles and Thomas, to confess. They had sworn an oath of secrecy to their brother at Bestwood Park in the Midlands, a week before Midsummer Night, when they were invited to join in a plot to advance the Catholic faith. They were told that Lord Grey and George Brooke were to be participants.[8] Midsummer Night was chosen because it was a 'collar day' on which most of the important people of the realm would be gathered together at Court wearing their regalia, especially the Lord Keeper of the Great Seal who would be instructed to arrest the King and Council and take over the Tower of London. They were hoping to raise a force of 1,000 men, but would have been happy with 500.

Lord Cobham* and Sir Walter Ralegh were the principal figures in the Main Plot and it was William's task to build up a case against them. By August 1603, William Waad was able to report to Robert Cecil that their enquiries had implicated Sir Walter Ralegh and Lord Cobham in a more serious plot which was to destroy 'the King and all his cubs'.[9] Waad spent many days at the Tower of London examining the suspects. Letters to Ralegh, who was now in the Tower, were intercepted by William Waad and sent to Cecil.[10]

James had no particular liking for Ralegh, and though the evidence against him him was not strong, there was certainly a case to answer, especially when his friend Cobham turned against him. A Walter Penycocke had been arrested and found to be carrying letters in his doublet, as well as letters hidden in his cloak, which were from Lord Cobham to the Count of Aremberg, the ambassador from the Spanish Netherlands.[11] With this evidence, plus the replies to his questions from George Brooke and Watson, Waad felt that he had enough material to report to the Privy Council. He asked Cecil for the details of Watson's first examination since he felt 'there may something be picked out of them'. The separation of all this complicated evidence into the serious Main, and the less important Bye Plot, was a major coup for William Waad. His detective work was excellent. Ralegh's evidence to William was contradictory. He said he knew nothing of Cobham's link with Aremberg, but finally admitted to being offered 8,000 crowns by Cobham, so that after frequent interrogations, Waad managed to produce a case against

---

* *Not* Sir Henry Cobham (1537-1592), the resident ambassador in France, known to William Waad.

him. Ralegh was eventually indicted at Staines on September 21, 1603, that:

> 'he did conspire and go about to deprive the King of his Government; to raise up Sedition within the realm; to alter religion, to bring in the Roman Superstition and to procure foreign enemies to invade the kingdom. That the Lord Cobham, the 9th of June last, did meet with the said Walter Ralegh in Durham House, in the parish of St. Martins in the Fields, and then and there have conference with him, how to advance Arabella Stuart to the crown and royal throne of this kingdom'.[12]

The Tower of London
John Stowe 1600

While they were both imprisoned in the Tower, Ralegh tried to communicate with Cobham to persuade him to change his accusations. He even implicated Gawen, the son of the Lieutenant of the Tower, Sir George Harvey, by asking him to pass messages between them. Sir George Harvey had been specifically installed in the Tower by Robert Cecil to enable him to obtain the 'right' evidence to convict Ralegh, but Harvey had failed miserably, and he was in imminent danger of being cashiered. A series of pleading letters from Harvey to Robert Cecil and King James, reveal the depths of his unhappiness.[13] Eventually, Harvey redeemed himself by holding back a retraction signed by Cobham which would have negated the accusations against Ralegh, although by this time William Waad had been called in to extract the necessary information from Cobham.[14] This meant that Robert Cecil had his evidence and a court case could take place, although its location was switched from London to Wolvesey Castle in Winchester, in Hampshire, because the Plague was still raging in London. Waad, who had first been the interrogator of Ralegh, now became his guardian, before becoming his gaoler.

It was Waad's task to make sure that Ralegh was brought safely to his trial. On November 10, Sir William accompanied Ralegh by coach to Winchester. Some of Ralegh's friends waited along the route to wish him luck, but generally people were hostile. In fact, Waad feared a riot. He wrote, 'if one hare-brained fellow amongst so great a multitude had begun to set upon him, as they were near to do it, no entreaty nor means could have prevailed; the fury and tumult of the people was so great'. It took them two days to reach Bagshot, in Surrey, and another three days to cover the remaining thirty miles to Winchester. The wardens, fellows and students of Winchester College had been instructed to vacate their apartments for the expected influx of noblemen, judges and officials. Ralegh seemed very relaxed, calmly smoking his pipe and taking little notice of the crowds waiting to meet him. Waad was taken by surprise at the huge crowds, particularly in London, who showed little fear of the Plague in order to surround Ralegh's coach:

> '...it was hab or nab whether or not he should have been brought alive through such multitudes of unruly people as did exclaim against him. He that had seen it would not think there had been any sickness in London'.[15]

While Ralegh was still on his journey those implicated in the Bye Plot were being tried. First the two priests, then George Brooke and Sir Griffin Markham, with other lesser conspirators, were tried on November 15, and all found guilty apart from Sir Edward Parham who Waad had first questioned three months before. Two days later it was the turn of Ralegh, to be followed by that of Cobham and Grey.

The court was held under the King's commission of Oyer and Terminer,* and the commissioners were some of the most important men in the land. These included Sir William Waad as well as the professional lawyers, Lord Chief Justice Popham and Chief Justice Anderson. Wolversey Castle had been specially converted for the trial. Under a brocaded canopy in the centre of a raised platform sat the Lord Chief Justice with the other justices on either side of him. Opposite them sat Sir Edward Coke, the Attorney General, who was to lead the prosecution. The trial lasted from eight in the morning until seven in the evening, and began with the indictment giving details of the correspondence between Ralegh and Cobham, including the financial assistance they hoped to get from Spain amounting to some six hundred thousand crowns. Ralegh pleaded not guilty. Sir Edward Coke, the Prosecutor, was the same man who had prosecuted Essex and Southampton for treason, a very able lawyer who was to become one of the greatest judges in English legal history. Coke, however, was particularly bitter throughout this trial calling Ralegh a monster with an English face but a Spanish heart. Cobham called Ralegh a villain and traitor, and blamed Ralegh for instigating the plot and urging him on. Then Cobham claimed that Sir William Waad had tricked him into making accusations against Ralegh:

> 'that villain, Wade, did often solicit me, and got me, by a trick, to write my name upon a piece of white paper, which I, thinking nothing, did; so that, if any charge came under my hand, it was forged by that villain Wade, by writing something above my hand, without my consent or knowledge'.[16]

This accusation by Cobham that Waad doctored the evidence by obtaining his signature on a blank sheet of paper is highly likely. Waad was well known for his devious practices during interrogation. He was also known to open prisoners' letters, and make copies of the contents before resealing them. Waad had confessed as much in 1602 when pursuing Jesuits.[17] Such practices were routinely used by the intelligence services.

Although Cobham was in the same building, Sir Walter was

---

* Oyer & Terminer – To hear and to determine.

not allowed to confront his accuser. The prosecution used written evidence from Copley, Watson, George Brooke and others. During the trial the name of Captain Keymis came up again and again, as it was claimed that he had carried messages from Ralegh to Cobham when they were in the Tower. Keymis was a friend of Ralegh who, although probably innocent, had been deliberately implicated by the authorities in order to build a case. Ralegh complained to the commissioners that Keymis had been threatened with the rack, even though the King had ordered that 'no rigour should be used'. Waad had to admit that, although he had never actually threatened Keymis with the rack, he had told him that he deserved it. This revelation embarrassed the commissioners who claimed that they knew nothing about it. This method of eliciting information was commonly used by Waad and others. The mere mention of the 'rack' seems to have turned many a strong man weak at the knees. The most important evidence against Ralegh was given by Cobham who had made several statements and several retractions. He did state, however, that Ralegh was to be given a pension of £1,500 from Spain.[18]

As was usual in government trials of this period, the result was inevitable. Most of the commissioners were dependent upon King James, so the hand-picked jury took only a quarter of an hour before bringing in their guilty verdict. The two priests, Watson and Clarke were executed on November 29 and George Brooke on December 6. Brooke is thought to have been a double agent, and as such the link man between the Bye and Main Plots. As the younger brother of Henry Brooke, Lord Cobham, Warden of the Cinque Ports, George had not inherited any of the family fortune so was forced to make his own way in life, the suggestion being that some of his income came from intelligence. Yet, despite his co-operation with the authorities, George was not spared the block. His sentence was not commuted as he mounted the platform, a common practice used by the government to both terrify and save agents. So when Brooke realized that he was doomed he began to declaim people in high places.[19] Unfortunately, Brooke had the misfortune of being Robert Cecil's brother-in-law which meant that Cecil could not be seen to give him preferential treatment, even if he had considered it. On November 29, 1603, six days before his execution, George

Brook wrote in desperation to the King beseeching him to speak to Sir William Waad 'to whom (having been his late charge) I have imported more than to any other'.[20] Waad could not save him either, because of course he was working for Cecil.

The King signed warrants for Cobham, Grey and Markham to die on December 10. Ralegh's date of execution was fixed for December 13. At the last minute however, most of these sentences were changed, some of them on the scaffold as the prisoners awaited their fate. Markham and Copley were exiled, Grey and Cobham were imprisoned. Ralegh was sent to the Bloody Tower on December 16 to remain a prisoner for the next thirteen years. William was to become his gaoler from 1605.[21]

Although the spotlight remained on internal divisions and conspiracies the Secret Service was still keeping a close eye on anyone linked with Spain.

Notes

1 DNB, Robert Devereux, 2nd Earl of Essex (1565-1601).

2 CSP Domestic Addenda 1580-1625, p.399.

3 APC Oct. 28, 1601.

4 Prisons: Wood Street Counter (or Compter), a debtors' prison in the City of London EC2; Newgate Prison, near St. Paul's; The Tower of London; The White Lyon in Southwark; and The Fleet was near Fleet Lane in the City.

5 C. Northcote Parkinson, p.52.

6 HMC XVIII and CSP Domestic, 1603-1610 passim.

7 Recusancy in the North, Nov. 1603, Algernon Cecil, *A Life of Robert Cecil, First Earl of Salisbury,* (London 1915) p.374.

8 HMC Vol. 23 Addenda 1562-1605, after Aug. 3, 1603, p.113: HMC Pt XV Markham's Confession Aug. 14 and 15, 1603.

9 CSP James I 1603-10, Aug. 23, 1603.

10 ibid 1603-1610 passim.

11 HMC XV, p.228.

12 ibid 1603-1610 p.72 Jan 31, 1604.

13 ibid 1603-1610 passim.

14 Dixon, *Her Majesty's Tower,* p.367 calls Waad 'an evil genius' who was sent to the Tower to invent a method of connecting Ralegh with the Arabella Plot (Bye & Main Plot).

15 CSP Domestic, James I Vol. IV p.76.

16 DNB and Weldon, p.350.

17 CSP Domestic James 1601-3, May 1, 1602 Barnes to Charles Paget.

18 Cal.Patent Rolls, Edward VII Vol. 2, Nov 10, 1552.

19 Francis, *Guy Fawkes*, p.57.

20 HMC XVII, p.294.

21 In Oct. 1995, documents were unearthed in the Bodleian Library which provided evidence that Raleigh wanted Spain to invade Britain, and had asked for a Spanish pension of £1,500 p.a. in return for spying and denouncing King James. Until this discovery the case against him had been thought weak.

Sir William Waad's house at the Tower, on Tower Green,
now called The Queen's House.
Historic Royal Palaces

CHAPTER FOUR

LIEUTENANT OF THE TOWER

ALTHOUGH KING JAMES HAD shown some gratitude to Sir William Waad for all his work and dedication during the time of Queen Elizabeth, he had not yet sufficiently rewarded him for work in the early months of his reign when Waad had been involved in the discoveries associated with the Bye and Main Plots. Rewards of land had been very acceptable, but Waad was hoping for something more important, something with status and power attached to it, and this finally came on August 16, 1605[1] when Sir William Waad became the new Lieutenant of the Tower of London. He was, 'a man of good discretion, great fidelity and full of care and diligence' according to the Earl of Dorset who did not know 'a fitter man' to fill the post.[2]

Waad succeeded Sir George Harvey who had died in office just five days previously. Harvey's son, Sir Gawen, attributed his father's death to the 'troubles of his office, which had hastened his father's end', following the disgrace of the Ralegh/Cobham inter-lude since when Sir George had been under considerable strain. Waad was sworn in by the Lord Treasurer, and received an inden-ture of all the prisoners who were lodged in the Tower and all the 'percusites' to the Lieutenant's house. This was not an easy post. Sir Gawen was relieved to hand over the responsibility as he told Waad that he had hardly slept during the previous six nights.[3] Waad knew that his new authority brought with it the hatred of many in-carcerated there, so he would have to be on his guard. He knew that the evidence he had assembled had been used to convict Lord Cobham and Sir Walter Ralegh so he was unlikely to be popular with them. Before signing for his prisoners Waad checked on their presence. Surprisingly, their initial reaction to him was relatively neutral. Lord Cobham was sullen. The other prisoners' reactions were similar, except Sir Walter Ralegh who 'used some speech of his dislike of me'. This was understandable when 'that Villain Waad', as Ralegh called him, had assisted Cecil by securing the doubtful evidence against him. Despite this, Ralegh, ever the gentleman, apologized for his rudeness when Waad visited his prisoners the next day. Lord Cobham's fury, however, had not abated. He was so abusive that Waad gave orders for him to be locked up in his lodging. Cobham ranted and raved in such a loud voice that people in the courtyard heard it, much to Waad's annoyance. The next day Cobham had calmed down and even apologised to Sir William who seemed happy to forgive him but confided to Cecil, 'I did heat myself so upon Thursday by going to all the prisoners that since I find myself exceedingly distempered'.[4] At not far short of sixty years of age, the new Lieutenant of the Tower found these visitations and confrontations very distressing.

Sir William had only three months to settle in before the problems of the Gunpowder Plot overtook the routine of the Tower, and during that time one of his chief distractions was the behaviour of the lions. The Tower was not just a prison but a Royal Palace, Armoury and Mint. It also contained the Menagerie, which had been established in the thirteenth century, and was as fascinating to King James as it was to all other visitors. During one visit James set three hunting dogs, one at a time, onto a dominant male lion to test their relative strengths, and gave orders that, after the killing of the first two dogs the third should be saved and removed from the lion's cage.

The lions' quarters were situated just west of the middle tower where they had a yard surrounded on the east by a semicircle of dens. The yard was paved with Purbeck stone and the lions were let out to exercise in the yard through wooden doors which could be raised with rope and pulleys, by drawing the doors up between stone openings. There was a large cistern where the lions could drink, and their quarters consisted of two storeys so that the lions could move between the lower and upper room. Wooden channels on tilted floorboards took the animals' urine away to a central point in the lower dens. The lioness had just 'whelped' in a shed which had been built for her in the yard.[5] Waad enjoyed this pleasant distraction from his more serious duties and frequently reported to Cecil on their progress.

Though fascinated by these creatures held captive in the Tower, Waad's main responsibility was to his prisoners. After a few days in office he wrote a full report to Cecil. Sir William was a stickler for detail. Upon arrival at the Tower, he had received a warrant stating the limit of liberty and access to his prisoners, but he soon found that many of his prisoners had more privileges, and much more liberty, than they were allowed. There was also a high degree of laxity in the prison regime. High-ranking prisoners were allowed their own servants but, 'Lord Cobham had one servant more than was allowed', and many unauthorised people had open access to him as Cobham's prison door to the roof was open all day. Waad was indignant that Cobham's visitors even used a private staircase through his, the Lieutenant's lodging, to gain access over the roof to the prisoner, but he soon remedied this by shutting doors and posting guards. Sir Walter Ralegh gave him even more cause for alarm. His report continues:

> 'Sir Walter Ralegh has like access of divers to him, the door of his chamber being always open all the day to the garden', and adds wryly, 'which indeed is the only garden the Lieutenant has'. Not only that but, 'in the garden he has converted a little hen-house to a still-house where he spends his time all the day in distillations'. Waad did not wish to move him but would like the use of his garden and to regain some privacy because at the moment he was overlooked by Ralegh in both house and garden, 'none can come to the house but he espies them on all sides', and suggested the building of a brick wall 'where the pale* now stands, and the walls raised very little, which would not be above 20 marks charge'.

Lord Grey, he remarks, was in the same cell where he was

---

* Pale – fence.

examined. There is no access to him, but he does have the freedom of 'all the King's lodgings, and the door to those gardens, by
which, when the King was there, my Lord Chamberlain came to
his lodgings'. Lord Grey had been pressing Waad to allow 'Lady
Goring and the Lady Fleetwood his near kinswomen to visit him'
which was previously permitted, but Waad found 'no authorisation
for this'.

Even the prison warder seemed to be in league with Grey,
which Sir William soon rectifies, but with the other prisoners he
reports, 'I find as yet no fault but that they are well kept'. All these
problems with high-ranking prisoners must have been quite testing
for Sir William who seems to have been suffering from 'ague', or
malaria, at this time. He claims to have had 'three fits' already by
August 22.[6]

Waad is seen as a new broom determined to crack down on
the leniency in the prison and bring in a new, tougher regime; he
was not prepared to be ruled by his prisoners no matter how high-
ranking they were. He did make changes, and he did try to restore
the privacy of his own garden, but asked for guidance about 'such
liberty as shall be thought fit to be granted them'.[7] The Council's
reply to Waad's request for more detailed instructions, advised him
that the King was prepared to be a little freer on the point of access.[8] The King and Council were particularly keen to give Waad
greater authority over his prisoners to make them fully aware that
Waad was their keeper, and that it was he who would report to His
Majesty, using his own judgment about the disposition and treatment of his captives.

Sir Walter Ralegh was undoubtedly Waad's most difficult prisoner at this time due to his popularity with the public, not to mention Queen Anne's and her son, Prince Henry's great admiration
for him. Waad objected to Ralegh's arrogant attitude and decided
to control his freedom of movement. Infuriatingly, even after Waad
had demolished the wooden fence on his property and built a wall
to give himself more privacy, Ralegh had the nerve to walk up and
down on top of the wall smoking his pipe and acknowledging the
affection of curious citizens who thronged to see this handsome,
dazzling figure.[9] Sir William retaliated by introducing a curfew in

the late afternoon after which time prisoners were to be kept in their rooms and not allowed their customary freedom. Nor were prisoners allowed to fraternize in the evening or dine with company. To drive home the message Waad set about evicting Lady Ralegh and her children, from the Tower where she frequently stayed with her husband, compelling her to rent lodgings nearby on Tower Hill beside Barking Church.[10] Waad was furious that she swept into the courtyard in her coach as if she owned the place. To prevent traffic entering the Tower, he commanded that carriages should stop outside the gates and not enter the grounds. It sounds petty, but in this clash of personalities between the flamboyant Ralegh and the more pedestrian Waad, Sir William was determined to assert his authority. Not all his actions were negative however, as during his lieutenancy many improvements were made. He provided extra accommodation for Ralegh by inserting a floor into his living space. A conversion in Beauchamp Tower provided Cobham with a study, and new windows were provided for Lord Grey. Waad was paid for some, but not all, of these changes and improvements. He also added a floor into the Great Hall of his own lodgings and raised the roof forming 'a great chamber with a fair bay window', where later he was to erect an important monument. It was into this room that Waad would later bring the conspirators to be questioned, one by one, before Northampton* and the Commissioners.[11]

It did not take Waad more than a few days in his new job before he quarreled with the Lord Mayor and Aldermen of London who were in the practice of voiding the city ditch into the Tower ditch and polluting its water. Much of the water came from the occupants of the multitude of houses built on the side of the Tower ditch, 'base people that keep swine and feed them with offal', according to Waad. He complained that the stench was so great that it made him ill.[12] This was just the first of many rows over territory he would have with the Mayor who continued to harass him for many years.

Many of the warders Waad inherited with his position were undesirables, 'some bankrupts, some given to drunkenness and dis-

---

* Henry Howard (1540-1614) Earl of Northampton.

39

order and most of them very ungovernable'. As with other areas of government life, it was possible to buy and sell positions; therefore those appointed often did not work but merely appointed a deputy. Because Sir William wanted men he could trust, he provided a list of five men who had served him for a long time with proven fidelity, whom he wanted to serve him – Robert White, William Jefferis, William Mills, Reynold Langhton, Humfrey Samster, as well as a certificate for three other men – William Crooke, Thomas Ravening and John Strebranck.[13] The Lieutenant also requested the services of some of his servants to assist him – like his friend John Lorcason, who had been Commissary of Musters in the Low Countries, and Samuel Wade, a relative who was the Under-Steward of the Court Leet of the Tower. After numerous clashes with the Gentleman Porter, Sir William Worthington, Waad eventually succeeded in replacing him with a Mr. Carew. The Gentleman Porter, technically in charge of the gates, was really the Deputy Lieutenant. Waad was so incensed with the insolent carriage of this man who refused to obey his orders, that he suspended Worthington with instructions that he should keep to his lodgings until 'the pleasure of the Lords be known'. All these changes meant that Waad had gathered around him a group of trusted men upon whom he could rely unreservedly. He was now prepared for future events.

Notes

1 HMC XVII, p.368 acceptance letter.

2 ibid, note xxxix clears up the discrepancy on the exact date of appointment; ibid, Dorset to Salisbury Aug 16, 1605, p.375.

3 ibid Aug. 10, 1605, pp364-376 Sir Gawen Harvey to Salisbury and Harvey to Salisbury Aug. 17, 1605,

4 HMC XVII, p.376.

5 ibid, p.402.

6 ibid p.377 and p.384.

7 ibid p.378.

8 ibid Council to Waad, Sep. 1605, p.443.

9 ibid Waad to Salis. Dec. 9, 1605.

10 Dixon, p.372.

11 ibid p.371/2.

12 HMC XVII, pp.387 & 402.

13 HMC XVII, p.644, undated but endorsed '1605'.

The Gunpowder Plotters showing eight of the thirteen conspirators:
Missing are Digby, Keyes, Rookwood, Tresham and Grant.
National Portrait Gallery

CHAPTER FIVE

THE GUNPOWDER PLOT

O<small>F ALL THE PLOTS</small> against both Queen Elizabeth and King James that had passed through the hands of Sir William Waad, the Gunpowder Plot was to become the most famous.

A country's religious faith is not established overnight but during hundreds of years, so when Henry VIII overturned the religious applecart in 1534, he threw the populace into a turmoil which existed not only under the short reigns of Edward (Protestant), and Mary (Catholic), but well into Elizabeth's time. After centuries of Catholic worship, the English were now asked to become Protestants, a change that was strongly resisted by the ancient families of the landed-gentry who could afford to pay the recusancy charges imposed by the state. The rest of the country either conformed, or appeared to do so, by attending Protestant church services to avoid paying the fines. Therefore, during the reign of Queen Elizabeth I, there were practising Protestants in the country, but also two bodies of Catholics existed in England at the same time.* The English Catholics were ancient families who had always worshipped that way, although they considered their allegiance was to the monarch rather than the Pope; the Roman Catholics were converts and variously called, 'papists' or 'Romanists'. These men had been drawn into the religion by Jesuit priests entering England from training colleges on the continent. They saw the Pope as their supreme leader and their country as Spain, not England. Roman Catholics' apostasy was seen as a protest against the state and/or against family; in other words, a show of political or personal dis-

---

*There was also a group of Puritans who felt that Elizabeth's reforms had not gone far enough.

sent, often by angry young men. The Roman Catholics were few but English Catholics were many – estimated to be about half the population; one third of these were peers of the realm, half were country gentlemen, and the rest were 'lesser classes'.[1]

Fathers Robert Persons and Edmund Campion were the first senior Jesuits to enter England, in 1580, against the wishes of the English Catholics. Their mission was to stir up dissent in England and reclaim the populace for the Italian church – a treasonable act. Persons who became the first English Prefect of Jesuits, was said to have reclaimed the Tresham and Catesby families before he returned to Rome. Father Weston then stepped into Persons shoes as Prefect. Later he was thrown into the Clink Prison where he was interrogated by William Waad before being taken to the Tower, convicted of treason and put to death. Henry Garnet then became the new Prefect. Garnet settled near London in Enfield Chase to be near his lay supporters, and to receive the helpers Fathers Fisher, Gerard, Oldcorne and Tessimond (alias Greenaway) among others, who were then sent to the Midland shires to begin their missionary work. In order to hide themselves from the authorities the Jesuits used many guises and many false names.[2]

In the other camp were supporters of the English Catholics, like the priests William Watson and William Clarke who denounced the foreign school and intended to rout the Jesuits from the country. This feud between the secular English Catholics and the Jesuit, Roman Catholics was fierce, with each ready to betray the other on the slightest pretext, a situation Robert Cecil was quick to turn to his advantage.

The year before Queen Elizabeth died, Father Garnet, the Superior of Jesuits in England, received two papal letters, one addressed to lay Catholics and the other to the clergy. These letters insisted that Catholics should *not* support or tolerate any successor to the throne of England who was not a practising Roman Catholic.[3] These letters had come via Flanders through the Papal Nuncio, who had instructions to pass them to all English Catholics when the Queen died. Crucially, Father Garnet later admitted under interrogation that he had shown these letters to the three leading protagonists in the Gunpowder Plot: Catesby, Percy and Wintour.[4]

Although Garnet claimed to have destroyed the papal letters upon the uncontested accession of James, these letters would have had a powerful effect on recusants as they appeared to give tacit papal support to any dissident action. Garnet had also heard of plans by the Pope and the Spanish and French kings to set a Roman Catholic upon the English throne when Elizabeth died. These plans came to nothing but Catesby, Percy and Wintour must also have known this fact through Garnet.

By now Robert Catesby was already well-known to the authorities as a leading figure in the Essex Rebellion, when he had been wounded and taken prisoner. He had escaped relatively lightly from this brush with the authorities by paying a fine of £3,000. This had meant that he had to sell one of his estates, but he was still hungry for action in the Catholic cause.[5] At this time he was a good-looking thirty-year-old, over six feet tall with noble bearing and manners to match, a natural leader but wild, a liar and gambler with a constant debt problem.[6]

Exactly like the perpetrators of the Bye and Main Plots, and in view of what they thought they knew about the attitude of France and Spain towards non-Catholic monarchs, early in 1603 Robert Catesby, William Parker (the fourth Lord Monteagle) and Thomas Percy decided to appeal to Spain for help. Thomas Wintour eventually went as an emissary, first to Flanders, and then to Spain. Next went Christopher Wright and Guy Fawkes. They tried to convince the ruler of Spain, King Philip III, that a new invasion would have the support of Catholics, but there had been a regime change in Spain and unlike his father, Philip III was not interested. Instead he wanted peace with England and would not consider their request.[7] William Parker was playing with fire as he was already on Cecil's blacklist due to his involvement in the Essex Rebellion. He would play a controversial part in the affairs that followed.

Robert Catesby was one of those becoming impatient with the state of affairs following the accession of King James. After the failure of the Bye and Main Plots, which he must have watched with interest, early in 1603 Catesby began to devise his daring plan to blow up king and parliament using gunpowder secreted under the House of Lords. One important factor in the preparations for the plot was to ensure that only those persons who needed to know were told, therefore initially the plotters were confined to a small number of co-related individuals.

CONSPIRATORS - FAMILY CONNECTIONS

Catesby, Tresham, Wintour, Vaux:

1st Lord Vaux of Harrowden

Sir George   m.   Catherine   2nd Lord Vaux
Throckmorton   Vaux   of Harrowden

                                      3rd Lord Vaux

Sir Robert Throckmorton   Catherine   m.   William   (m1)   (m2) Mary Tresham
                           Throckmorton   Wintour   dr. of Sir

                                                                Thomas Tresham

                           George Wintour
                       (m.1) Jane   (m.2)
                             Ingleby   Anne
                                                      Vaux

            Robert   Thomas   Dorothy   John Wintour
            Wintour   Wintour   m.
                                John Grant

Muriel   Anne
m.   m.
Sir Thomas   Sir William
Tresham   Catesby

            Robert
            Catesby

Francis   Frances m.   Elizabeth m *Lord Monteagle*   Mary m. Th. Habington
Tresham   *Lord Stourton*   of Hindlip

Percy, Ward, Wright

Thomas   Marg.   Marmaduke m Ursula   **Jack**   **Christopher**   *Martha* m. **Thomas**
Ward   Ward   Wright   **Wright**   **Wright**   *Wright*   **Percy**
                                                                       m.
            Mary Ward   Margaret Ward

Robert Keyes' mother, and **Ambrose Rookwood's** father, were brother and sister (Tyrrwhitt)

Obviously both a royal hostage and a senior nobleman would be needed to give credibility to this band of renegades, once the first part of the plan had been implemented. However, there seems to have been considerable confusion among the conspirators over which of the royal children should be kidnapped following the 'blow'. Initially the conspirators considered abducting the eldest child, Prince Henry, but as they assumed that he would attend par-

45

liament with his father and be blown to pieces, they then agreed that Thomas Percy should seize young Prince Charles, and Catesby would abduct the nine-year-old Princess Elizabeth who was staying at Coombe Abbey, near Coughton Court, the home of the Catholic Throckmorton's in the Midlands.[8] Four-year-old Charles was discounted as being too young to be of use, although on the birth of baby Mary she was considered a possible target because she was the first royal child born in England.[9] In the end they settled on abducting Princess Elizabeth. As far as a Protector* was concerned, none of the conspirators seem to have made a firm decision on this, although the authorities believed that the Earl of Northumberland was their choice for this role, as he was regarded as the unofficial head of Catholics in this country.

According to the government-approved version of events, the chronology of the Gunpowder Plot was as follows:[10] early in 1604, the mission to obtain support from Spain having failed, Robert Catesby began to implement his plan. His first move was to arrange a secret meeting with Thomas Percy, a distant relative of the Henry Percy, the Earl of Northumberland, who acted as Northumberland's steward and rent collector in northern England. Then Catesby outlined the plot to John Wright and Thomas Wintour (or Winter) at his house in Lambeth. These three were the nucleus of the conspiracy.

Thomas Wintour was a servant of Lord Monteagle. John or Jack Wright, and his brother, Christopher or Kit, were related to Thomas Percy by marriage through their sister Martha. Thomas Wintour and his brother Robert were related to the staunch Roman Catholic Vaux family of Harrowden, and to the Throckmorton family through marriage, and indirectly related to Robert Catesby. Both Wintour brothers had also been at school with Guy Fawkes in York.

Following this meeting, Catesby sent Wintour to Flanders to try to persuade Velasco, the Constable of Castile, to press for good terms for English Catholics in the forthcoming peace negotiations to be held shortly in London at the behest of King James. Catesby also asked Wintour to bring back Guy Fawkes, his old school chum

---

* Protector – a regent in charge of a kingdom during the minority of a sovereign.

who was serving as a soldier in Flanders. Fawkes had been a servant to Lord Montague.

In April 1604 Guy Fawkes and Thomas Wintour landed back in England with glum news. The Constable had dashed their hopes of a reasonable settlement for Catholics in the forthcoming peace agreement. This meant that the plotters now abandoned all hope of a legitimate resolution to the issue and decided to proceed with their plan.

On May 20, 1604 all five plotters (Robert Catesby, Tom Wintour, John Wright, Guy Fawkes and Thomas Percy) met at the Duck and Drake in St. Clement's parish off the Strand where Thomas Winter usually stayed when in London.

A few days later the same group met again at a house near St. Clement's Inn and all five took a solemn oath on a 'primer' or prayer book. All of them then heard mass in another room, and took the sacrament from Father John Gerard who, according to statements taken from Fawkes and others after capture, was not told of the plan.

On May 24, 1604 Thomas Percy connived to use his privileged position as a Gentleman Pensioner* to take over the lease of a single bed-roomed house called Vinegar House, adjacent to the Lords' chamber, from John Whynniard, Keeper of the Old Palace of Westminster. He then handed the keys of the house to Guy Fawkes.[11] Catesby's friend, Ambrose Rookwood, was then asked to purchase some gunpowder which was stored in Catesby's house in Lambeth, on the other side of the River Thames, but Rookwood does not appear to have been told about the plot at this time.[12] Robert Keyes, who had been a servant to Lord Mordaunt, was recruited as a caretaker and to work on a proposed tunnel from beneath Percy's lodging to below the parliament chamber. Now there were six plotters.

The idea to construct a tunnel, or 'mine' as the authorities called it, seems very impractical and unnecessary. It would require the removal of soil and rubble, and the need to import wooden beams to shore up any supposed mining operation. Thomas Percy and Robert Catesby were known to have been tall men (Catesby

---

* A type of royal bodyguard.

over six feet). They were also gentlemen who would not have dirt-ied their hands by tunneling, even with the help of Robert Keyes. In addition, Percy's lodging was surrounded by occupied buildings; therefore they were in constant danger of being observed in their operations.

Historians have suggested a number of reasons for this episode being included in the official history of events. The best supported of these is the Elizabethan love of drama and symbolism. In this instance, the tunnel is synonymous with evil. It is underground, a symbol of the forces of darkness. The men who created it are there-fore tainted and likened to creatures of the nether regions of earth, unfit to walk above ground like ordinary men.

At the time the plotters were working to a deadline when Parliament would reconvene, but, due to the arrival of the Plague in the capital, parliament was prorogued until February 7, 1605. Therefore the plotters allegedly stopped work and reassembled in early December 1604 when a seventh plotter, Thomas Bates, ser-vant of Catesby, was recruited. The Scottish commissioners then took over Percy's Crown Property lodging, Vinegar House, for their meetings on King James's pet project at this time, the proposed union of Scotland and England. So, according to the official version there was no work on the tunnel until just before Christmas. The gunpowder was assembled and brought over the river by boat from Lambeth to Percy's house. Gunpowder was not difficult to find and could be bought anywhere. Pilferage seems to have been rife, as in December 1600, William Waad and others were asked to look into 'the problem of abuses committed by officers of the ordinance con-cerning the misuse of powder and munitions committed to them'.[13] Nor was the use of gunpowder an original idea as a murder weapon – the original proposal to kill Queen Elizabeth I involved placing barrels of gunpowder in the apartment below her bedroom.[14]

The Peace Treaty between England and Spain, signed in July 1604, which made possible the recruitment of Englishmen to sup-port the Catholics (the Spanish cause) in the Low Countries, was of considerable advantage to the conspirators who could now use this as a cover for the accumulation of gunpowder, weapons and horses needed for the second part of the plan.

They assembled again on December 11, 1604, allegedly to complete the tunnel up to the wall of the foundations of Parliament house. At this point Chris Wright was recruited as a labourer so that, according to the government view, by December 24, 1604 the tunnelers had reached the Parliament House and dispersed for Christmas. This brought the total number of plotters to eight.

In early January 1605, John Grant and Robert Wintour were brought into the conspiracy. John Grant was another relative. He was married to Robert and Thomas Wintour's sister Dorothy. Grant later brought in his friend Henry Morgan who was to be involved in the subsequent 'hunting party' following the explosion. But for now there were ten plotters.

During February 1605 Parliament was again prorogued until October 3, 1605, this time because of plague in some counties. According to official sources it was really prorogued because James's planned union of England & Scotland was creating many administrative and legal difficulties, or was it actually prorogued because Robert Cecil was not ready?

So for two weeks, we are told, the conspirators tried to tunnel into the parliament building through the massive foundations, but found the work impossible due to the thickness of masonry. By a stroke of luck, the authorities would have us believe, Ellen Bright, the tenant of the ground floor vault below the Lords' Chamber, vacated the premises, and Percy managed to obtain the lease from the Keeper of the Palace, John Whynniard, on March 23, 1605. As this gave direct access to below the chamber, the plotters now abandoned the tunnel and dispersed again.

All these delays were costing Catesby money because at this time he was funding the whole project, so he and Percy decided to try to recruit new men of wealth from the Midlands area they knew so well. Their targets were Ambrose Rookwood, Sir Everard Digby, and the Littletons. The Rookwood family were wealthy Catholic trouble-makers even during Elizabeth's reign. The Queen had quite deliberately descended on their house at Euston Hall in 1578 during one of her progresses and remained there long enough to seriously deplete their coffers. This had ensured that the family was effectively neutralised for several years.[15] Rookwood was a horse-breeder and kept a stud at Coldham Hall. He did not provide money but would be useful in providing animals for the 'hunting party' at Dunchurch following the 'blow'. Sir Everard Digby was a convert to Catholicism who is believed to have contributed £1,500.[16] Both these men were told that the plot had been sanctioned by Jesuits. Stephen Littleton, and his cousin Humphrey, of Holbeach, were told that they were raising troops for the Catholic Regiment in Flanders. Mrs. Vaux of Harrowden, a devout old-school Catholic, was asked to invite other squires to meet the plotters.

In May 1605 Fawkes sailed to Flanders where he told Hugh Owen about the Plot. Owen was an elderly, multi-lingual Welsh spy who had fled England after he had supported the claims of the Isabella of Spain to the throne of England.[17] Owen was to advise Fawkes's military commander in the service of Spain, Sir William Stanley, and in September Sir Edmund Baynham[18] was to inform the Pope. The plan was to call in Stanley for help after the explosion.

By the end of August 1605, Fawkes had returned to England. Ambrose Rookwood and Sir Everard Digby were then told, and finally Thomas Tresham was told. Tresham was useful because of his money – he had guaranteed £2,000 – but Catesby was not entirely confident of Tresham's total devotion to the cause. The number of conspirators had now risen to thirteen. Fawkes and Wintour then put fresh gunpowder in the vault as they felt the original powder may have decayed.

Parliament was prorogued yet again on Oct. 3, 1605 for another month, so the plotters decided to leave London. Perhaps to release the tension in these days leading up to the event, or as a cover for their meetings, the conspirators held a number of suppers in various inns around London to which they invited guests. On October 9, the playwright Ben Jonson was one of those guests at the Irish Boy in the Strand.[19] On October 26, 1605 Catesby and Fawkes returned to White Webbs in Enfield Chase, the home of the Vaux family which was used by Father Garnet and the Jesuits. Here they learned from Wintour that King James's son, Prince Henry, would not be attending the opening of parliament.

On October 27, 1605 Wintour received a hurried visit from

Thomas Ward, a servant of Lord Monteagle, who told him some disconcerting news about an anonymous letter that had arrived for his master which appeared to give the game away.[20] Wintour sped hot-foot to Catesby with this information and urged him to abandon their plans, but Catesby wanted to 'wait and see'. Fawkes was sent to check the cellar to see if it had been disturbed. When he did, everything appeared in order. Catesby and Wintour, who had never trusted Tresham, accused him of leaking details of the plot, a charge he vehemently denied. They believed him.

On November 3, 1605 Percy returned to London. After discussion they all agreed that the plan was still on, and Percy dined with his master the Earl of Northumberland.

What happened next is probably known by everyone who has studied British history. According to the authorities' version of the event, 'at dead of night on the 4th November going into the early hours of the 5th November 1605, Guy Fawkes, using the name of John Johnson, was caught in the act, with all the equipment on his person, ready to blow up the parliament building and most of the important people in the realm, including the King'.

The House of Commons' Journal for November 5, 1605 records the main event:

'This last Night the Upper House of Parliament was searched by Sir Thomas Knevett; and one Johnson, Servant to Mr. Thomas Percy was there apprehended; who had placed 36 Barrels of Gunpowder in the Vault under the House with a Purpose to blow the King, and the whole company, when they should there assemble. Afterwards divers other Gentlemen were discovered to be of the Plot'.

Bonfires burnt brightly in the streets of London that night to celebrate the deliverance of the King.

Notes

1 Seel & Smith, *Crown & Parliaments 1558-1689*, p.27 & Dixon, p.38.

2 Dixon, Vol. II, p.32 onward.

3 PRO SP 14/19/41 and 42, *Investigating Gunpowder Plot*, Nicholls p.69 'who did not set forward the Catholic religion ....and according to the customs of other Catholic princes ....submit himself to the see apostolical'.

4 Later, under questioning, Garnet admitted that Mr. Catesby had built all his intentions upon these 'breves'. HMC XVIII, p.87.

5 Chastleton Estate, Tessimond, p.54.

6 Tessimond, p.61.

7 PRO SP 14/19/94; Nicholls pp 38/39.

8 Dixon, p.141/2.

9 Fraser Antonia, *The Gunpowder Plot*, p.117.

10 The Official Version of the plot appears in the first collection of the Works of King James which was published during his life-time by Mountague, Bishop of Winchester. Although attributed to James it was an official government document and, as such, was probably compiled by Francis Bacon.

11 Vinegar House – Dixon, p.125 onward.

12 At this point, Rookwood claimed he did not know how the gunpowder would be employed. He is said to have purchased two or three barrels. Rookwood's examination and admission, PRO SP 14/216/126/136.

13 Records of the Privy Council, Dec. 1600.

14 CSP Spanish, 1587, Mendoza to Spanish King.

15 Northcote Parkinson, p.52.

16 Trials, p.30.

17 Archduchess Isabella was the much-loved daughter of Philip II of Spain.

18 Sir Edmund Baynham was a malcontent who had been a conspirator in the Essex rebellion and was admitted by Fawkes & Wintour in their statements to be a 'sleeper' who would explain the act to the Pope upon its success; PRO SP 14/216/163, 170; also Sprott, 'Sir Edmund Baynham' p.1.

19 Fraser p.149. Jonson was a recusant, who although not thought to be aware of the plot, was brought before the Privy Council when he offered his services to Salisbury in an attempt to assist the authorities and save his reputation.

20 Monteagle was Francis Tresham's brother-in-law. He was married to Francis's sister Elizabeth. Contents of the letter appear above.

TEXT OF THE MONTEAGLE LETTER

My lord out of the loue I beare to some of youere frends I have a caer of youer preseruacion therfor I vould aduyse yowe as yowe tender youer lyf to deuyse some exscuse to shift of youer attendance at this parleament for god and man hathe concurred to punishe the wickednes of this tyme and thinke not slightlye of this aduertisment but retyre youre self into youer contri wheare yowe maye expect the euent in safti for thowghe theae be no appearance of anni stir yet I saye they shall receive a terrible blowe this parleament and yet they shall not seie who hurts them This councel is not to be contemed becaus it maye do youe good and can do yowe no harme for the dangere is passed as soon as yowe have burnt the letter and I hope god will giue yowe the grace to mak good use of it to whose holy proteccion I commend yowe

My lord, out of the love I bear to some of your friends I have a care of your preservation, therefore I would advise you as you tender your life to devise some excuse to shift of your attendance at this parliament, for God and man hath concurred to punish the wickedness of this time, and think not slightly of this advertisement but retire yourself into your country [county] where you may expect the event in safety, for though there be no appearance of any stir yet I say they shall receive a terrible blow this parliament and yet they shall not see who hurts them, this counsel is not to be condemned because it may do you good and can do you no harm for the danger is passed as soon as you have burnt the letter and I hope God will give you the grace to make good use of it, to whose holy protection I commend you.

Addressed to: The right honourable

The Lord Monteagle

PRO SP 14/216/2

CHAPTER SIX

THE AFTERMATH

The need for a search was obvious after Monteagle had shown the anonymous letter to Robert Cecil (now Lord Salisbury)* who eventually showed it to King James on his return from a hunting expedition in Royston, Hertfordshire. But Salisbury did not show any urgency in advising the King after the mysterious letter had been delivered to Lord Monteagle's house at Hoxton, in North London, on the night of October 26, 1605. A stranger delivered the letter to one of Monteagle's servants, who then handed it to his master. Monteagle asked a servant, believed to be Thomas Ward, to read it out aloud before taking it immediately to the authorities. Ward knew Wintour and was distantly related to the Wright brothers, thus maintaining the circle of friends and relatives implicated in the plot. Though King James took the credit for uncovering the meaning of the letter, if Salisbury knew of the existence of the plot, which most historians believe that he did, he was well aware of what was planned and could decipher the contents himself. Salisbury's action in allowing the King to discover its meaning was merely a political stratagem.

We will probably never know who wrote the Monteagle letter. Some historians believe that it was Tresham, because he had expressed concern to Catesby and Wintour about friends and family being blown to pieces, especially his brother-in-law Lord Monteagle, but Tresham never admitted this in his confession; others believe that Salisbury wrote the letter himself. However, it is

---

* Robert Cecil was made Earl of Salisbury on May 4, 1605. From this date onward letters and official documents refer to him as 'Salisbury' and so shall we.

much more likely that Monteagle was the author, as he stood the most to gain by disassociating himself from the conspirators after his involvement with previous plots.[1] Monteagle even received a grant of land, valued at £200 for his 'services in the detection of the Gunpowder Plot',[2] and although his name appeared in almost all the chief confessions, 'a tiny slip of paper was pasted over his name in every document produced in court' later.[3] Another theory investigated by Waad, was that the warning letter might have been sent by Percy, because Monteagle owed his wife £500 which would have been lost if Monteagle had been blown up.[4]

Waad, writing on November 5, thanks God that all his prisoners are safe but then shows a hint of prior knowledge – 'My care hath of late been the more because we have been extraordinarily warned by such accidents as I told your Lordship, and the night watches are the severest of any fort in Christandom'.[5] Quite what this warning was, is never properly explained but it certainly sounds as if they knew that something was about to happen. Waad had obtained permission to appoint a further ten warders, and was later granted payment for their wages of 14 pence per day and liveries. The letter requesting these men is undated, perhaps deliberately so, but is likely to predate November 5, because even without prior knowledge of the plot, a new lieutenant was likely to want his own trusted men around him. His newly-appointed family friend, John Lorcason, would also play a prominent part in the proceedings.[6]

Once news of the plot broke there was tremendous activity. Waad felt that he should warn the authorities about the public's simmering resentment against the Spanish residents in London who were suspected of being behind the plot. Sir William was prepared for the worst and told Salisbury, 'because I know all the gates of London are kept, I have brought all the warders into the Tower, and set a watch at the posterns and Gate of St. Katherine and at the landing strands'.[7] He was delighted that the plot had been foiled. 'I thanke God on the knees of my soul that this monstrous wickedness is discovered; and I beseech God all the particularityes may be layed open and the traitorous wretches receive their desserts.'[8]

The Gunpowder Plot, though more dramatic than many of the previous plots to destroy the monarchy and restore the Catholic faith, depended on two essential elements, firstly a dramatic gesture like the murder of the king, and secondly, the organisation and collection of a considerable group of committed men, who would assemble and respond once the initial act of rebellion had taken place. The organisation of this fighting-force was disguised under the cloak of a hunting party. To throw off suspicion, Catesby claimed that the full stables and assembled weaponry were intended for the Low Countries where Catholics could now support the English Regiment in Flanders, following the Peace Treaty with Spain.[9] Even after the discovery of the store of gunpowder, and failure of the first part of the plan, Robert Catesby and many of his supporters foolishly tried to continue with the second part, which was destined to end in dismal failure.

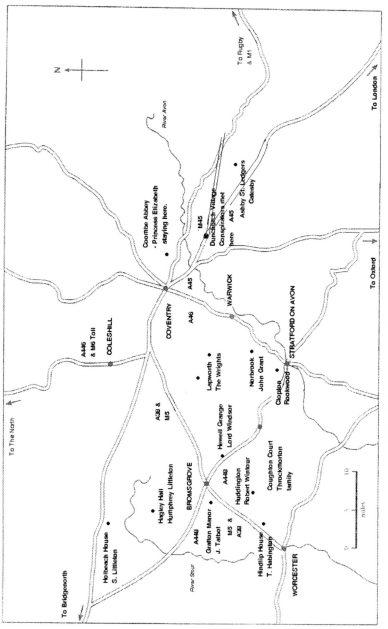

Map of Midlands showing location of homes of conspirators.

After his arrest Guy Fawkes, or John Johnson as he called himself, was interrogated by the king. He gave little away, but did admit that the cellar in which he was arrested belonged to his master, Thomas Percy, so the hunt was on for Percy. In fact it was Sir William Waad who gave the first correct information about the whereabouts of Thomas Percy. Confusion reigned during these first few hours as Popham told Salisbury that Percy had escaped towards Gravesend in Kent, whereas Archbishop Bancroft reported him fleeing south towards Croydon, commenting that 'all London is up in arms'.[10] But Waad had found him, and wrote yet another letter to Salisbury on November 5:

'It may please your good lordship my cousin Sir Edward York, being lately come out of the north and coming this afternoon to me, upon speech of the happy discovery of this most monstrous plot, he telleth me he met Thomas Percy, the party sought for, going down to the north disguised... From the Tower in haste'.[11]

Fawkes, who was not intimidated by the King, by Coke, the Attorney-General, or Popham, the Lord Chief Justice, was then taken to the Tower to become Sir William's prisoner. His cell was kept locked and he was guarded every night. The King sent a list of questions to be put to Fawkes. He gave permission for the rack to be used, but suggested that this should be used as a last resort with the gentler, but still horrific, punishments being used first.[12] This meant the manacles – suspension by iron gauntlets from a wall by the wrists. Suspects could then be left dangling for hours on end – a system Waad had used many times before.

Once at the Tower, Waad examined John Johnson, who had in his pocket a letter addressed to Guido Fawkes, but could get nothing from him. He was totally silent and would not respond to questions, so Waad decided to try again the following morning. He was astonished at Fawkes' calm reaction to his hopeless situation, 'who hath taken such rest this night as a man void of all trouble of mind'.[13] But Fawkes was a Protestant convert to Catholicism,* and as such a fanatical and zealous Roman Catholic, who so believed in his mission that he felt slaughter was justified in order to promote

---

* Fawkes had been baptised and initially raised as a Protestant.

the cause. Here was a man like Christopher Waid, the Marian martyr of Dartford; Fawkes too would have kissed the stake to which his effigy would later be attached and burnt at countless bonfires across the country for centuries to come. Waad reminded Fawkes that the State would not be prepared to accept his silence, telling him quite openly that unless he was instructed to the contrary he would continue to interrogate him until 'I had gotton the inwards secret of his thoughts and all his complices'. 'Prepare yourself for torture' he advised him, 'if this becomes necessary'.[14] Despite the methods used, Guy Fawkes managed to keep the authorities guessing for some days to enable the other conspirators to escape, or carry out the second part of their plan.

Next Waad tried to find out if Fawkes was bound by an oath of secrecy made as a sacrament. Although Fawkes held out for some time, he eventually confessed that he had made a solemn vow and received the sacrament upon it. He had promised that he would perform the act and not disclose it, nor give the names of any of his friends. He admitted that his vow had been made in England some eighteen months previously, and said that he didn't know what torture might make him say but he was resolved to keep his vow. He did state that the priest who had given him the sacrament, a Father Gerard, knew nothing of the intended plot. When Mr. Corbett, one of the Clerks of the Council arrived, Waad asked Fawkes to restate his answers in his presence and having drawn so much out of him, he decided not to press further on that occasion, 'for then he would conceive I took advantage upon his confession to deal more rigorously with him'. Waad was a skilled interrogator and knew when to turn the screw; there was plenty of time as the interrogation would continue for many more days. Fawkes told Waad that, 'since he undertook this action he did everyday pray to God he might perform that which might be for the advancement of the Catholic faith and saving his own soul'.[15]

Waad reported that Fawkes was in 'a most stubborn and perverse humour as dogged as if he were possessed'. He had promised to give them a full account of the plot but had now changed his mind. He was 'so sullen and obstinate as there is no dealing with him'. Though concentrating on Fawkes, Waad mentions to Salisbury his suspicions of Lord Arundel, Sir Griffin Markham, and Tresham, 'long a pensioner of the King of Spain', as possible suspects.[16]

By the next day Waad was able to inform Salisbury that he had persuaded Fawkes to disclose 'all the secrets of his heart', to his Lordship only, 'but not to be set down in writing'.[17] This letter suggests that Fawkes should confess to Salisbury alone, before pen was put to paper. After the Ridolfi plot in 1571, a decision had been made *not* to allow prisoners to write their own confessions but to dictate them instead.[18] This gave the authorities considerable scope to alter the facts. The resulting document was then copied out by the prisoner, if he was still capable of writing; if not, it was just signed. Waad was elated and added, 'he will conceal no name or matter from your Lordship to whose ears he will unfold his bosom. And I know your Lordship will think it the best journey you ever made upon so evil occasion'. Waad was now confident that he could procure the complete truth by degrees and gain Fawkes's signature to a confession. The use of the rack finally loosened his tongue so that Fawkes gradually began to name names. His distorted signatures on various documents bear witness to the extent of his suffering.

The rack was a much feared instrument of torture which consisted of a large, oblong, wooden frame, raised from the ground on short supports. The prisoner was attached by his wrists and ankles to rollers at each end of the contraption. A system of levers and ratchets then stretched the unfortunate prisoner, very slowly and painfully dislocating his body in the process. Over a period of several days Fawkes made several confessions. An important one made on November 7, 1605, was witnessed by Sir Edward Coke, Sir William Waad and Edward Forsett.[19]

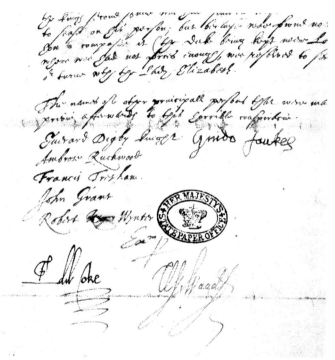

The last page of Guy Fawkes's confession showing the signature of Sir William Waad and several conspirators, including Guido Fawkes.

Transcript of Guy Fawke's confession. (extracts).

This page.............

Concerning Duke Charles, the King's second son, we had sundry consultations how to seize on his person, but because we found no means how to compass it – the Duke being kept near London – where we had not forces enough, we resolved to serve ourselves with the Lady Elizabeth.

The names of other principal persons that were made privy afterwards to this horrible conspiracy.

(signed) Guido Fawkes
Everard Digby, Knight
Ambrose Rookwood
Francis Tresham
John Grant
Robert Wynter
(witnessed) Edward Coke (Attorney-General)
W.Waad (Lieutenant of the Tower of London

While Fawkes was holding the authorities at bay in the Tower, the main group of conspirators was gathering around Holbeach House in Staffordshire where everything was going wrong, and even the weather was against them. Soaked by a torrential down-pour, tired and confused, they insanely attempted to dry some gun-powder in front of an open fire. In the resulting explosion Catesby, Rookwood, John Grant and his friend Henry Morgan were seri-ously injured. In fact Morgan was so badly burnt that he lost his sight. Some conspirators were beginning to flee, but Tom Wintour returned to Holbeach. A large force under the High Sheriff of Worcestershire, Sir Richard Walsh, soon surrounded the house and in a shoot-out with both crossbows and muskets, many of the conspirators were wounded or killed, including their charismatic leader Robert Catesby. According to reports, Percy and Catesby, fighting back to back, were both killed by the same shot. Some, including Grant and Morgan, Rookwood and Tom Wintour, were captured, but most were shot down and later stripped of their pos-sessions by the locals in a savage fashion.[20] While Percy's master, the Earl of Northumberland, was placed under house arrest in the temporary care of the Archbishop of Canterbury at Lambeth Palace, the remaining plotters and suspects were gradually rounded up and eventually transferred to the Tower of London, as was allegedly eighteen hundredweight of gunpowder which was removed from under the Palace of Westminster.

There is much speculation about this gunpowder. The Jesuit, Father Francis Edwards,* believed that the barrels did not contain gunpowder at all, but had been substituted with soil instead, and that knowing this, Sir William Waad and his cronies rowed upstream from the Tower to collect the barrels and removed them, first emp-tying the soil outside the building under cover of darkness, which gave rise to the tunnel myth.[21] Bishop Goodman, writing only forty years after the event, even asserted that he had seen this soil with his own eyes and wrote as much in his memoirs.[22] As Lieutenant of the Tower, Waad was also in charge of armaments, and indeed large quantities of gunpowder were already stored at the Tower. How better to lose a suspect shipment of barrels which may contain something else? We only have the authorities' word that the barrels they removed from the vault did indeed contain gunpowder, and

---

* Father Frances Edwards S.J., author of Guy Fawkes.

there is the evidence that Sir William had already recruited some "trusted men" to assist him in his task of managing the Tower at this time. Was this why Salisbury was so relaxed about the impending 'blow'? Did he know there was no danger from barrels of soil, decayed powder or even empty barrels?

For any insurrection to be successful, a powerful nobleman would be needed to act as figurehead. The most prominent man associated with this plot was the Earl of Northumberland, who according to the authorities was the unofficial head of Catholics in England, and Percy's distant relative. Initially, he was held under house arrest at Lambeth Palace until the authorities decided how to handle the situation. The Earl was first examined in depth on November 23 and then moved to the Tower on November 27 [23] where he joined many other suspects including the Catholic peers, Lord Montague in the Constable Tower; Lord Mordaunt, who had 'fallen into an extreme pensiveness, not without great cause' and Lord Stourton, both in the Brick Tower with a view over Tower Hill to the Minories and St. Catherine's.[24] Known troublemakers, leading recusants and Catholic sympathisers were rounded up. Salisbury was determined to link the plot with the Jesuits, so Catholic houses were searched where priests were known to hold secret masses. These included White Webbs, near Enfield, which was raided on November 11. Secret hiding places were revealed, but Father Garnet was not found. It took the authorities nine days to search the huge Vaux house at Harrowden. Elizabeth Vaux eventually showed the searchers some hiding places and thus diverted attention from the room where Father Garnet was hidden, but in the end she was taken away for questioning. Many other houses were searched and some ransacked, with wives, servants and friends being questioned.

Waad and others were to spend months examining not only the conspirators, but anyone who might have had links with the plot. Waad knew that it was the small details which could be important when added to other facts, and had managed to find out that Fawkes' mother was still alive and married to a man known as Foster, an obstinate recusant. He had also learned that the two Wrights, Fawkes and the Jesuit Tesimond had been at school together. Waad's attitude is summed up in the sentence, 'I am bold to advertise every little occurrence which gives light to further discovery'.[25] So thorough was he that he wanted to examine some of the scarves cast aside by the conspirators in their haste to flee. He felt that if the embroiderers could be found they might provide information about when they were made, and for whom.[26]

Thomas Wintour was also questioned by Waad. This statement which was signed by Wintour, and was published by the authorities, has been considered suspect for many years, not least because there are suggestions that Waad may have replicated the method he used with Cobham during the Bye and Main Plot, when he allegedly persuaded Cobham to sign a blank piece of paper.

Questioning continued even after the execution of the main conspirators at the end of January 1606. But, one conspirator who did not need to be put to death was Francis Tresham who is believed to have died in Waad's custody, but there is considerable controversy about the fate of this conspirator. In his letters Waad appears to be very concerned for Tresham's health. He told Salisbury on December 15, 1605, that he had appointed a nurse for him, but that 'Tresham is worse and worse, tomorrow I have appointed a consultation for him of three doctors'. But no copies of any of the reports by these doctors survive. Waad's next statement is curious, 'If he escape it must be by great care and good providence that he may die of that kind of death he most deserveth'.[27] It would appear that Waad is anxious for him not to die in his bed so that he may suffer a traitor's death, but is there more to this than meets the eye? Waad was well-versed in the use of coded language through his training as an intelligencer. Was he instead referring to a planned escape, engineered by Salisbury, which would enable Tresham to live a normal life and die a normal, natural death elsewhere, which he deserved to do after his service to the authorities? Father Edwards believes the word 'escape' is the key word here and that, for his services to Lord Salisbury as an informer, Tresham did indeed quit the Tower with the assistance of the authorities. There are even reports of Francis Tresham and his brother William being seen in their flight to the continent, although this may be a case of mistaken identity.[28] Eight days later on December 23, he is said to have died in great pain, according to the authorities, from a strangury.* Waad sought advice on what to do with the body. But here is another anomaly, because according to the authorities he had lain so long dead that the body was beginning to decompose and needed to be disposed of quickly, 'because he smelt exceedingly when I was with him yesterday in the afternoon' according to Waad. He was also concerned that the body would be 'begged', for burial by the family. Tresham's friends, who believed him dead, were not slow to point the finger of blame at the authorities.[29] There are reports that an eminent Cambridge doctor who visited him, diagnosed poison as the cause of death.[30]

However, Waad also wrote, 'I find his friends were marvellous confident if he had escaped this sickness and have given out words in this place that they feared not the course of justice'.[31] They no doubt expected him to be tried, found guilty and saved from the gallows in the nick of time, like many collaborators before him, but not to die in prison. If Tresham was the agent-provocateur many historians suspect him to be,[32] then it is possible he was spirited away, because if he were pardoned or escaped a traitor's death this would throw considerable suspicion upon the government's involvement in the plot. Indeed Tresham is known to have received a 'passport', or licences to travel abroad for two years with servants and horses. This was granted on November 2, 1605. He did not try to abscond before the fateful November 5, so was he making arrangements to quit the country after the event with the blessing of the authorities? There is certainly something very strange about his relaxed attitude after the discovery of the plot and arrest of Fawkes, as Tresham did not go to ground nor did he show any fear or expectation of being arrested after the event, but remained openly at large in London for a week before the authorities caught up with him.[33]

On the other hand the passport could merely have been a sop to pacify Tresham who was subsequently arrested and disposed of. Death in custody was an easy option – men were known to die under torture, or he could be said to have contracted an illness. Salisbury described it as 'a natural sickness such as he hath a long time been subject to', but this could be a cover story.[34]

---

* A blockage or irritation at the base of the bladder.

A copy of Tresham's supposed dying confession which was taken down by either his wife, or servant William Vavasour, was found recently at Deene Park, the home of Thomas Brudenell who had married Mary, sister of Francis Tresham.[35] In this document, Tresham retracted a previous statement implicating Garnet by his 'being acquainted with Wintour's employment in Spain', which stated that both Father Garnet and Father Greenway had been present at their Enfield Chase meetings.[36] The new document stated that he had not seen Garnet for sixteen years before the plot. This was clearly not true, so here Tresham appears to be appeasing his conscience. Copies of Garnet's treatise on equivocation were later found in Tresham's rooms, to the great joy of Coke who used them at Garnet's trial.[37] Vavasour was held prisoner after the statement was taken so, conveniently, it never saw the light of day, although in Waad's letter to Salisbury on December 15, 1605, he asks if Salisbury wants to see it, saying that it was delivered 'sealed up'.[38] This suggests that the authorities were aware of its existence, but appear not to have acknowledged it. There is yet another twist to this convoluted tale as according to some reports, as yet unproven, Vavasor was reputed to have been Sir Thomas Tresham's base son.[39] Certainly, for public consumption Tresham was treated as a traitor even though he had never been indicted. His head was to be struck off and exhibited on a spike in Northampton. Whichever version is believed, it is worth noting that according to tradition, the heads were parboiled and then tarred, to enable them to last longer, making them virtually unrecognisable. The exact whereabouts of the rest of his body are unknown. Perhaps the only two people who knew the truth about the Tresham affair were Waad and Salisbury.[40]

Sir Everard Digby, Robert Wintour and John Grant left the Tower on January 30, and were put to death with Thomas Bates, who had been held in the Gatehouse. The remaining four original conspirators were executed at Old Palace Yard, Westminster on the following day. These were Tom Wintour, whose confession Waad had supervised, Ambrose Rookwood, Robert Keyes and the final victim Guy Fawkes himself who had to be helped up the ladder, but at least he died quickly as his neck was broken by the fall. All of them were to suffer the prescribed gruesome treatment for traitors – hanging, drawing and quartering. They were taken through the streets of London to the place of execution by being 'drawn on a wicker hurdle' (a kind of stretcher) to be hanged, but cut down alive. The body was then opened, the heart and bowels plucked out and private members severed from the body 'before their eyes'. The head was then cut off and the body divided into four quarters 'to be disposed of at the King's pleasure'.[41] Heads were usually displayed on a spike above a wall or gateway, as a warning to would-be traitors.

Only two written confessions survive from the trial of the conspirators, one by Guido Fawkes which is undated, and the other by Thomas Wintour, dated November 23, 1605. Both are suspect.[42]

Notes

1 Guy Fawkes' statement of Nov. 16, 1605; also DNB 2005 online version Tresham.
2 CSP Domestic, James I, 1603-1610, Apr. 1606, p.314.
3 Dixon, p.196.
4 HMC XVII, p.550.
5 CSP Domestic, James I, Nov. 5, 1605.
6 Waad refers to John Lorcason as a 'cousin'.
7 HMC XVII, p.10.
8 GP Plot Book No.12.
9 The Peace Treaty with Spain was signed on August 19, 1604, at Somerset House.
10 GP Plot Book No. 13 & 14.
11 ibid no.14.
12 SP 14/216/37.
13 HMC XVII, Waad to Salisbury, Nov. 7, 1605, p.47.
14 HMC XVII, Waad to Salisbury p.479.
15 ibid.
16 GP Plot Book 48B; CSP, Waad to Salisbury, Nov. 8, 1605.
17 CSP, Waad to Salisbury, Nov. 9, 1605.
18 Ridolfi Plot 1571 – to take Queen Elizabeth I, dead or alive, free The Queen of Scots, set her on throne with Duke of Norfolk as consort and restore the Catholic religion, all with Spanish Army assistance.
19 GP Plot Book No. f.111.
20 Dixon p.189: 'stole their clothes … caused them to expire in…agonies of bleeding, thirst, and frost'.
21 Edwards Francis, S.J., *Guy Fawkes, The Real Story of the Gunpowder Plot?*, p.149/150.

22 Goodman, p.103.

23 Hatfield MS, 113/50, Lane to Salisbury, Nov. 28, 1605.

24 HMV XVII, Waad to Salisbury, Nov. 26, 1605, p.514.

25 ibid p.550.

26 ibid p.511/2.

27 ibid. p.553.

28 HMC Salisbury XV, Dudley Carleton to Sir Thomas Edmondes from Calais, Dec. 1, p.397: 'Betwixt this and Bologne, I encountered two Englishmen, slenderly provided (with few belongings), and concealed themselves from me without speaking or answering whilst we changed horses, I suspect to be stolen. One of them looked like Francis Tresham, but speech is, he is in the Tower.'

29 Wake Joan, The Death of Francis Tresham, *Northamptonshire Past and Present, II,* 1954, p.40-1.

30 Goodman, p.107; GPB 2/11.

31 CSP James I, Waad to Salisbury, Dec. 23, 1605.

32 The Jesuit Father Francis Edwards, in *Guy Fawkes,* certainly believed him to be an agent.

33 Trials, p.40.

34 Sawyer E., *Papers of Sir Ralph Winwood,*Vol, 2, p.189.

35 Wake, *Northamptonshire Past and Present,* 2, p.40-41.

36 Dixon, p.197.

37 Garnet, *Treatise of Equivocation,* Bodleian, Laud MS misc. 655 possibly dated 1595.

38 HMC XVII, Dec. 15, 1605, p.553.

39 ibid Nov. 1605, p.527.

40 Edwards, p.207.

41 Mears, Kenneth J. *The Tower of London.*

42 HMC XVII, Waad to Salisbury enclosed the confession 'in writing of his own hand'. p.511.

CHAPTER SEVEN

WIDENING THE NET – FATHER GARNET AND THE JESUITS

B UT THIS WAS NOT the end of the Gunpowder Plot. The authorities were keen to link the organization of the plot to the leading Jesuit, Father Henry Garnet. As the plotters had been Catholics, if it could be shown that the Jesuits were responsible then so much the better for the Protestant government. Garnet was initially held in the Gatehouse at Westminster where his first examination was before members of the Privy Council on February 13, 1606. Sir William Waad was present as well as Popham, Coke and the Lords Northampton, Nottingham and Worcester, with the Earl of Salisbury. They began by making fun of Garnet whose relationship with Anne Vaux was certainly enigmatic, more like husband and wife according to most sources. The inquisitors made cheap points against Garnet by trying to suggest that he was her lover rather than her confessor.[1] At a later examination, when discussing a baby's christening, Waad suggested that the priest was surely also present at the baby's begetting. At first the examiners were baffled by Garnet's attitude on equivocation and were unsure how, or even whether, to continue. Eventually they began to see how the prosecution could be conducted. The next day – Valentine's Day – Garnet was moved to the Tower and into the hands of Sir William Waad, who was 'feared only less than Popham for his venom against Catholics'.[2]

Father Garnet knew all about Sir William Waad because his colleague Father John Gerard had been badly tortured by him in the Tower in 1599, when Waad tried to obtain more information about Gerard's superior. At that time the authorities were keen to catch Garnet for 'meddling in politics'; he was said to be receiving information from abroad which made him 'a danger to the State'. As the threat of torture did not produce the answers he wanted, Waad suspended Gerard in manacles by his hands and arms for hours on end, and because Gerard's feet touched the ground, the earth was dug out so that he could be made to suffer. Waad was furious when this did not make the priest talk. 'Then hang there until you rot off the pillar', he retorted. When they eventually stopped torturing Gerard, he and another prisoner managed a daring escape by sliding down a rope from the roof of the Tower to the opposite side of the moat where friends were waiting to help them.[3]

Garnet was not as physically brave as Father Gerard and feared the rack, but even after his removal to the Tower he was initially treated well, describing his room as 'a very fine chamber' where he dined well and supped claret with his meals. He found Waad reasonable in his treatment and questioning, but when they moved to the subject of religion, Waad became, according to Garnet, 'violent and impotent' (uncontrolled) in his speeches.[4] Although William appeared to be considerate in his dealings with Garnet, it was done for a purpose. Waad had daily meetings with Garnet's keeper, Carey, and trusted him implicitly to pass on the information he received from Garnet. Waad of course, kept Salisbury informed – 'it may please you to keep this scribbled letter because they are the very words the keeper delivers'.[5] Waad's method of extracting the information was to lock them both up together and to take away the key. Carey, Garnet's keeper, had been instructed to gain the confidence of his prisoner by suggesting that he might convert to the Catholic faith. Soon Garnet was entrusting him with messages to other prisoners in the Tower and to some of his friends outside. Most of these messages were delivered, but they had all been scrutinized first by Sir William Waad.

Waad knew that most of these letters would contain secret messages because he had caught Father Gerard using the same system before, when he was in prison. If the juice of a lemon was used, the writing would become visible when placed in water, or heated, whereas writing in orange juice would become exposed only when the paper was heated. In a letter to Anne Vaux, via an intermediary, Garnet sends thanks for 'two pairs of sheets...' and requests another pair of spectacles 'to see things far off; for to read I need not', but within the letter, there was a secret message written in invisible ink explaining what he has, and has not, admitted during his recent examination by the authorities.[6] In this instance, Garnet used lemon juice which has the property of being made visible by water, but as soon as the paper is dry the message disappears again until either dampened or heated, when the message reappears. This meant that the secret message could be reused for onward transmission and Waad's interception was not noticed. If Garnet had used orange juice the secret message would have remained visible after heating and could not be used again. Water would have completely destroyed the secret writing.[7] By this means Waad was able to monitor most of Garnet's correspondence, particularly letters to 'his man' Richard Fulwood, an administrator who seems to have acted as his agent, instructing him to confess nothing.[8] Waad told Salisbury that Fulwood, 'who is the only trusted man by the Jesuits', should be apprehended, but in this the authorities were unsuccessful as Fulwood fled the country.[9] Carey's apparent kindness to Garnet is shown when Carey placed him in a cell, with a special hole through to the neighbouring cell, which enabled Garnet to talk to Father Hall, the alias of Jesuit Oldcorn. Their secret conversation was being monitored by one of Waad's men, his old friend John Lorcason, and Edward Fawcett, one of Northampton's spies.[10] A similar system had been used by Waad in getting Lorcason to listen to the conversations of Robert Wintour and Guy Fawkes some weeks earlier. With this information, plus what was extracted from Garnet by torture, Salisbury was approaching his goal of linking the plot to the Jesuits. Garnet finally decided to confess the little he knew in order to show that he was not personally responsible for the organisation of the plot. But, as Salisbury wrote:

> 'whether Garnet lives or dies is a small matter, the important thing is to demonstrate the iniquity of the Catholics and to prove to all the world that it is not for religion but for their treasonable teaching and practices that they should be exterminated. It is expedient to make a manifest to the world how these men's doctrinal practice reacheth into the bowels

of treason and so for ever after stop the mouths of their ca-
lumniation that preach and print of conscience'.[11]

The net was closing in. Anne Vaux was arrested and taken to
the Tower where she was interrogated, and her answers compared
with those of her friend and confessor, Father Garnet.

When Garnet's trial took place on the March 28 at the Guildhall,
Waad delivered him there in a closed coach. The crowd was sur-
prised at this departure from the usual method of walking prisoners to trial, especially as men of much higher birth had not been
given this privileged treatment. They may have suspected that his
high status in the church was being acknowledged in order to make
an even greater example of him. It is unlikely that the coach was
needed because of Garnet's incapacity due to torture as he had not
been racked for quite some time before the trial. The Lieutenant's
explanation for Garnet's disablement was that it had been induced
by incarceration in the priest hole at Hinlip before his capture. Much
more likely, the use of curtained transport was to distance Garnet
from the largely sympathetic crowd that the Council feared would
show him their support.

Waad had a problem, because the trial was held at the Guildhall
which was within the jurisdiction of his hated adversary, the Mayor
of London. A place for the prisoner was provided, but none for
Waad, therefore a place had to be reserved for the Lieutenant, as the
acknowledged custodian of the prisoner, in a railed off area.[12] King
James was believed to be there too, but hidden from view. This was
a show trial designed to round off five months of enquiries and to
bring to an end the main investigation into the Gunpowder Plot. As
in most public trials of this nature, planned to fit conveniently into
one day, it was obvious that Garnet was going to be found guilty.
Though it might be difficult to convict him of treason, he could
certainly be condemned for misprision of treason – that is the failure to notify the authorities of a known treasonous act such as the
Gunpowder Plot. He was to tell Waad later, that if anyone undertook to kill the King he was not bound to confess it unless there was
proof to convict him. Much of the trial hinged upon the doctrine of
equivocation which had been devised by Garnet himself as a way
in which Jesuits and Roman Catholics could lie to the authorities

without damning their souls.* If a disguised Jesuit was asked 'are you a priest?' did he reply 'yes', and suffer the legal consequences, or 'no', and offend God by telling a lie? Equivocation involved using ambiguous or evasive language, which enabled the man being questioned to satisfy both God and the State. For example his reply might be that he was 'no priest', by which he meant that he was not a priest like those in the pagan Greek temples.[13] Waad must have cursed the doctrine (which had developed over the previous ten years) because it made his job as an inquisitor almost impossible. Shakespeare's 'Macbeth' hinges on appearance and reality, what is believed and what will actually happen. 'Equivocation' is a key word in the play and Shakespeare is obviously referring to Garnet, and perhaps jesting about his trial, when putting many of his references to equivocation into the mouth of the drunken porter. Garnet was known for his love of wine, and the 'farmer' Shakespeare refers to in Scene 3 was one of the aliases used by Garnet – 'an equivocator that could swear in both the scales against either scale, who committed treason enough for God's sake yet could not equivocate to heaven'.[14]

The trial was not the success the authorities had anticipated. People were not convinced, as they could see that Garnet was condemned only for concealing the treason he had heard in confession, which is why over five weeks passed before the sentence was carried out. During this time Waad worked on Garnet again, by depressing him through insinuation and trickery into believing that 'five hundred Catholics had turned Protestant' following his trial, in order to trap him into confessing more involvement in the plot, but it was to no avail.[15]

On Saturday, May 3, 1606, Waad escorted his prisoner from the Tower to his place of death. Father Garnet was to be dragged on a hurdle to St. Paul's churchyard for his execution. It is not recorded whether Waad found satisfaction in his task but certainly his wife felt great sympathy for Garnet. She said she would pray for him and told him, 'God be with you and comfort you good Mr. Garnet.'[16] Anne Waad would have met Garnet on the occasions when he dined

---

* Sir Edward Coke, the Prosecutor, regarded this as the art of lying as practised by Catholics.

with the Lieutenant at their house at the Tower, but it is also likely that Sir William's wife had leanings toward the English Catholic religion through her mother's influence.[17] Suddenly, Ann Vaux rushed out of the crowd and had to be dragged away as she tried to approach Garnet in the courtyard. Waad was at first stunned, then furious, as he castigated her gaoler who had orders only to allow Ann Vaux to watch Garnet's departure from a Tower window.

After his final prayers in Latin, Garnet was hanged with his arms firmly folded across his breast. According to the John Gerard 'Narrative', the onlookers at his execution were so sympathetic that they demanded he should not be cut down alive before quartering, but cried out, 'hold, hold', and one man even pulled his legs to speed his death. The enormous crowd in the churchyard, rather than showing excited satisfaction was mysteriously moved by his death.[18]

Even seven months after the failed plot, the questioning went on. Father Strange was interrogated, also Nick Owen, known to many by his nickname of Little John, the man skilled in the construction of priest-holes,* and Ralph Ashby, who may have assisted him, as well as Father Oldcorne. It is claimed that Owen had been brutally tortured and died after one bout of punishment, though the authorities claimed he had committed suicide by ripping open his stomach. When referring to Nicholas Owen and his 'bestial' torture in the Tower, Father Tessimond wrote:

> 'I would like to put a question to the slanderers themselves and in particular to the Lieutenant of the Tower, William Waad, who supervised the torture and invented this fable. Waad is a man utterly corrupt, his word is worth little but I would like to ask him during all the time he was torturing Owen, or on some other occasion during his imprisonment, he ever saw in him impatience of a kind to lead one to believe that even in desperation he could kill himself...
> ...does William Waad seriously expect us to believe that even after many days torture a man like Owen would abandon his hope of salvation by inflicting death upon himself?'[19]

---

* Priest-hole – a hiding place for a Roman Catholic priest during Protestant searches.

Tessimond's purpose was to discredit the authorities, and from the safe distance of Flanders he was able to make his point well. He also referred to Waad as 'a butcher'. Tessimond obviously believed that Owen's so-called suicide was invented by Waad and that he had been put to death. He felt that Waad was a liar – 'one could mention any number of lies invented by this man and put about to harm and dishonour Catholics'. Tessimond claimed that Waad had made a metal band to put around Nick Owen's stomach to prevent it from bursting during torture and letting out his intestines, but eventually the stomach did burst, the wound opening as if it had been cut.[20]

It was not until October 1608, when most of the examinations had been concluded, that Waad was able to place in the Lieutenant's quarters a large, marble memorial, which still exists. It consists of a central oval surrounded by four slightly smaller ovals at each corner, decorated with the arms of the examining commissioners, including those of Sir William himself. It gives an account of the conspiracy, and records those saved by the discovery of the Plot, listing the names of those who were executed for their involvement. Part of it, translated from a mixture of Latin, Greek and Hebrew, reads as follows:

'To Almighty God, the guardian arrestor and avenger – Who has punished this great and incredible conspiracy against our most merciful Lord the King, our most serene Lady the Queen, our divinely disposed Prince, and the rest of our Royal House, and against all persons of quality, our ancient nobility, our soldiers, prelates and judges; the authors and advocates of which conspiracy, Romanised Jesuits of perfidious Catholic religion, and by the treasonous hope of overthrowing the Kingdom, root and branch; and which was suddenly, wonderfully and divinely detected, at the very moment when the ruin was impending, on the 5th day of November, in the year of grace, 1605 – William Waad, whom the King has appointed his Lieutenant of the Tower, returns on the 9th October, in the sixth year of the reign of James I, 1608, his great and everlasting thanks'.[21]

The Gunpowder Plot Monument in the Governor's House, Tower of London.
Erected in 1608 by Sir William Waad
The monument includes the arms of:
Sir Robert Cecil, 1st Earl of Salisbury, Secretary of State
Sir Henry Howard, 1st Earl of Northampton
Sir Charles Howard, 1st Earl of Nottingham, Lord High Admiral
Sir Thomas Howard, 1st Earl of Suffolk, Lord Chamberlain
Sir Edward Somerset, 4th Earl of Worcester, Master of the Horse
Sir Charles Blount, Earl of Devonshire, Master of the Ordnance
Sir John Erskine, 2nd Earl of Mar
Sir George Hume, Earl of Dunbar
Sir John Popham, Lord Chief Justice.
Sir Edward Coke, Attorney General
Sir William Waad, Lieutenant of the Tower

Notes

1 Carswell, p.44.
2 Caraman, *Gunpowder Plot,* p.353; ibid p.348.
3 Caraman, *Autobiography of an Elizabethan*, p.111.
4 Carswell, p.355.
5 HMC XVIII, Apr. 17, 1606, p.113.
6 HMC XVIII, p.60.
7 Caraman, p.119.
8 ibid, p.113.
9 Carswell, *Henry Garnet & The Gunpowder Plot*, p.105.
10 Dixon p.193; CSP James I 1603-10, Feb.23, 1606.
11 Henry Garnet, p.376.
12 Gunpowder Plot Book, No. 216, and CSP James I, Mar.27, 1606.
13 Zagorin Perez, *Ways of Lying,* p.210.
14 Shakespeare, *Macbeth*, Act. 2, Scene 3.
15 Narrative, Henry Garnet 1555-1606, Caraman, p.421.
16 Edwards, p.241.
17 Cal of Pat. Rolls Eliz. 1572-75. Anne's mother "widowe of Sir Humphrey Browne Kt" was investigated in May 1574 *'for procuring priests to say mass and administer sacraments contrary to the Act of Uniformity'*.
18 Caraman, p.443, 438.
19 Tesimond Oswald, *'The Narrative of Oswald Tesimond alias Greenaway,* translated by Francis Edwards *p.199.*
20 Tessimond, pp198-201.
21 Monument in the Governor's House on Tower Green, Tower of London.

CHAPTER EIGHT

UNRAVELLING THE KNOTS

GIVEN THE HIGH LEVEL of intelligence activity that took place in Elizabethan and Stuart England, both within the country and abroad, it is hard to believe that the authorities were caught off guard by the Gunpowder Plot. Historians differ in their interpretations of the amount of involvement by Salisbury in the plot, from originator to manipulator, but there is little doubt that he must have known. Although both Burghley and Salisbury did cut back on secret service spending at various times throughout their respective offices,[1] the intelligence network still consisted of agents in the field sending back information. Perhaps, more importantly, in the case of the Gunpowder Plot, there were umpteen servants in countless households who contributed snippets about their masters' activities, for a small sum. This meant that the Stuart Secret Service was well-served to listen in on any developing plots following the succession of King James I.

There were letters in circulation which hinted at prior knowledge, one such by a self-confessed 'Katholyk' who hated the 'protystans relygon' with all his heart and yet could not consent 'to ether murdar or treson'. This man put his letters in a box and requested whoever found it to 'cary hit to the Kings magesty'. He appears to have been a servant of the recipient of an incriminating letter, who being a priest absolved him and made him swear never to reveal the contents to anyone. The letter is undated so it is not known if it arrived in time to warn the authorities.[2] However, one man who certainly knew something in advance about a plot was William Udall; whether or not Salisbury believed him is another matter. As a known informer, Udall had had a number of patrons;

up to 1608 his letters were addressed to Robert Cecil (Salisbury), after that date to Sir Julius Caesar, the lawyer and Senior Master of Requests in 1600. Udall claimed that he had given information to the authorities about the plot eleven months before it was discovered, and that Salisbury had treated the whole affair as a joke until a month before the intended fatal day:

> 'Yf the late Lord Tresurer had lived he used always to laugh at my offers. I offred to his Majestye (known to his greatest counsellors) the discovery of the Powder treason xi moneths before hand. My Lord Treasurer made a jest of the offer being continued by me til one moneth before the treason fell out (as I have letters to prove)'.[3]

Udall was a very strange man with whom Sir William Waad had experienced considerable aggravation when the spy had given evidence of the plot involving the late Earl of Essex and the Earl of Tyrone against Queen Elizabeth. Waad was unsure of Udall's allegiance because he had also been named by the priest Watson, so Waad kept him for a long period in the Gatehouse. Udall had been raised in the Midlands which meant that he knew both the area and its residents well. His early career as a spy had been spent in Ireland, where his wife's relations provided him with information. The Council in Ireland had sent him under guard to London because they did not know what to believe concerning his boasts about discussions with Tyrone, his claim that he had single-handedly brought down the Earl of Essex, and his vague assertions of plots to kill Elizabeth. Lord Mountjoy, one of his exasperated employers, later claimed that he 'fills me with a confusion of idle propositions'.[4]

Many spies and intelligence-gatherers like Udall spent time in prison, partly as a cover for their activities, but also because people like Mountjoy, and even Waad, were uncertain of their true allegiance. Although ambiguous and untrustworthy, they were still used by the authorities. These spies played a dangerous game, balanced on a knife-edge between Protestant and Catholic. They knew, as well as Salisbury and Waad did, that a change of monarch could mean their death or elevation, so their intelligence often seemed confused. It was Waad's job to unpick this web of half-truths to expose the nub.

As a prisoner in the Gatehouse, Westminster, Udall was an embittered man and desperately wanted his case to be heard. He had endured nineteen weeks of solitary confinement, and feared that his wife may have been murdered. Although Waad had examined him a number of times his case had not progressed. Four days later he was regarded as a dangerous criminal and bound to his bed for fourteen days. Waad, who at this time was busy with the trial of Ralegh at Winchester, claimed that he had not heard about Udall being put in irons or of his strict treatment, and said that he would be happy to receive letters from him, but when Waad received a letter at Winchester, and learned that it was from Udall, he had apparently refused to read it.

Letters from Udall read like chapters from a Dickensian novel. Towards the end of 1603, William Udall wrote to the Lord Treasurer of Scotland. He warned that his letters should not be shown to any Englishman, especially Waad, as Waad was only keeping him in prison because of Father Watson's evidence. Udall claimed that Waad was totally different when questioning a prisoner alone, than when others were present. For a man who claimed to have such love for his King, Udall certainly seems to have suffered: 'I have had since my close imprisonment for want of relief, four children perish, my wife lamentable murdered, carried out of her bed for dead and lay in an outroom all night alone. In the night she crept to her bed again and in the morning without all company was found dead in her bed... my children lay unburied till they began to savour'.[5] Waad was probably allowing him to fester in gaol in order to extract the truth from him.

After Queen Elizabeth's death, Udall claimed that he had informed the authorities when some men came to see him to advise him of a plot to kill James as he travelled south to London. Waad's problem was to decide whether Udall's evidence could be relied upon. Most people seemed to dislike and distrust Udall, but still clung to the scraps of information he offered. He even stated openly to members of the Privy Council that Thomas Strange had told him that Salisbury was one of those involved with the Main

Plot; a situation Udall had misread entirely as Strange was a Jesuit priest who was feeding him misinformation, perhaps in order to discredit any future, correct information Udall may pass to the authorities. Strange told him that Salisury and Raleigh planned to assassinate James on his way south to London and place Henri IV on the English throne – a ludicrous claim, certainly as far as Salisbury was concerned. No wonder Waad found it difficult to believe him. When arrested Udall made a plea to the King to set him free, but this time he had gone too far; because the authorities could not accept the treasonous claims against Salisbury, and he was sent from the Gatehouse at Westminster, to join the thieves and murderers in Newgate prison.

In the light of all this information, it would not be surprising if Salisbury did disregard Udall's claims about the Gunpowder Plot, but it is very unlikely that he did. Salisbury like Waad, was a highly organized, sceptical person who, even if he was mistrusting of both Udall and his intelligence, would still have investigated the claim. In fact, Udall was planted as a cook in household of Sir Everard Digby at the time of the plot, so that when the authorities conducted a massive sweeping up operation, to net all suspects immediately following the plot, Udall was one of those arrested.[6]

Other spies were also employed: Richard York was watching Ambrose Rookwood. Thomas Wilson, Salisbury's own personal intelligencer, watched White Webbs and the Vaux family.[7] Agents were always out there anyway, dogging the footsteps of Jesuits, watching their activities, noting who attended their masses and counting their numbers. It would appear that William Waad was also put onto the case. In fact, he already knew these men in Enfield Chase, in Warwick, in Stratford and in Dunchurch, as they had reported to him in the past.[8] He is said to have had been employed by Salisbury at this time as 'a wakeful spy and unscrupulous tool', to watch the two major conspirators, Percy and Catesby, which is why he knew exactly where Percy was when the hue and cry went up after Fawke's was taken.[9] As he had two charges to track down, he appears to have been using his friends and relatives to monitor their whereabouts. His years of experience in the field of espionage and counter-espionage had paid off.

A prolific letter writer all his life, Waad's letters to Salisbury were frequent, often long, and very detailed, but during the period 1603 until his installation as Lieutenant of the Tower of London in August 1605, there is a conspicuous dearth of correspondence from Waad. This is a particularly difficult period to research as a fire in the Whitehall Great Banqueting House on January 12, 1618, 'under which the Records of the Councell were kept', destroyed the Privy Council Registers from 1601 to May 1613.[10] In addition to this stumbling block is the probable deliberate destruction, or even non-existence, of letters covering the period of the Gunpowder Plot. All this lack of evidence of course encouraged the speculation which began to proliferate immediately after the plot, and continues to this day.

On the face of it, Waad seemed to be tracking down imported 'seditious' Catholic literature, hunting out secret Catholic printing presses, and searching for priests during this time, but what was he really up to?[11] Almost all of his correspondence at this time is sent from his house at the 'Ermitage'* at Charing Cross,[12] which suggests that he was mostly operating from within London and not journeying further to his house at Belsize. As the circle of conspirators widened, cracks appeared through which slid more of Salisbury's spies, ears and eyes wide open, ready to feed back information on the developments of the plot. By the beginning of 1605 most Catholic homes in the Midlands had been infiltrated. So much for the 'blow', but a secure plan needed to be in place to deal with the events immediately following November 5, and this is where Waad's experience and expertise as Muster Master General became extremely useful. If the conspirators had not been so engrossed in their own business, but opened their eyes as wide as Salisbury's spies, they would have noticed something unusual stirring in the countryside.

---

* The Hermitage – was part of the former St.Katherine's Hermitage close to the original Charing Cross, between Northumberland House and Scotland Yard (in what is now Whitehall). The 'Ermitage' was, conveniently, only a stone's throw away from parliament and adjacent to the Strand where Salisbury lived.

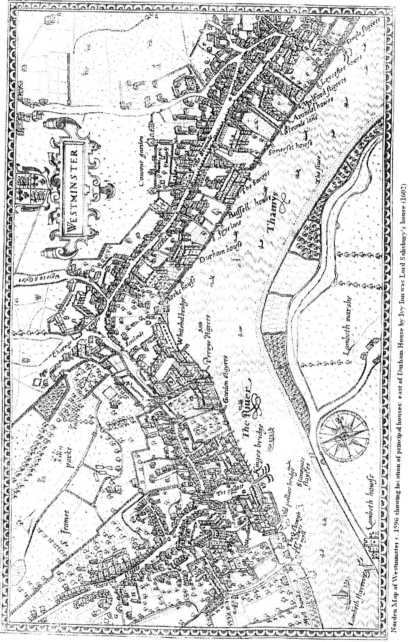

Norden Map of Westminster c. 1596 showing location of principal houses: east of Durham House by Ivy Inn was Lord Salisbury's house (1602)

As Clerk to the Privy Council, Waad had become Muster Master, when his task had been to collect information from every part of the country concerning the numbers of troops available in preparation for war in the run up to the Armada. At that time he had learned the importance of close contact with the Lord Lieutenants of the counties who provided vital information for their areas. After the danger of invasion had evaporated, Waad wrote a detailed paper on the measures necessary to protect the country from attack.[13] Many of these ideas were used in 1596 when a further threat to national security from Spain was met with similar preparations, and again he produced a thoughtful and detailed paper on the subject.[14] So successful were his ideas that he was made Muster Master General in 1598. In this post, his function was to co-ordinate the work done by the Lieutenancy. As England had no standing army Waad advocated the need for co-ordination and training as extremely important. Even if there was no immediate threat to the nation, the Head of State was always at risk. The systems Waad had put in place were now used for precisely this purpose – to protect the life of the King.[15] He certainly had plenty of experience in this field as he had also become Muster Master for Troops in the Low Countries in 1600 and Inspector of Irish Forces in 1603.[16]

During the summer and autumn of 1605 musters had been called among the trained-bands in the shires. In the counties the lieutenants were required to oversee these operations, while in the shires Privy Council members were given this task. Attention was focused on Warwickshire where Lord Compton, the King's Lieutenant, had received special instructions from Whitehall to review men and arms to ensure that everything was in readiness. A London armourer had been sent to supply guns and pikes to the Warwickshire bands who were preparing for action by practising in the fields near Norbrook.[17] In November 1605, the county would have been ready for any eventuality and could respond quickly.

Notes

1 Nicholls Mark, *Investigating Gunpowder Plot.*

2 HMC XVII, p.530-531.

3 Udall to Sir J. C. Lansdown, MS 153 ff 136 & 137, Doc. No. 42. July 17, 1612.

4 Harris, *Recusant History* Vol. 8 Reports of Wm. Udall, Informer.

5 HMC XV, p.296-7.

6 CSP James Vol. 216, No.47.

7 Francis Edwards, p.55.

8 Dixon, p.159.

9 ibid p.367.

10 APC 1613-14, p.v.

11 HMC XVII, Waad to Salisbury, May 22, 1605, p.216: & Aug. 3, 1605, p.350.

12 ibid, pp 101, 265, 350 1604/5; Ralph Aga's woodcut map of London mid. 16th c.

13 Birch Ms.4109 p.343, Mr. Waad's *Remonstrative Remonstrances When the Alarms of the Spaniard Approached.*

14 ibid, '*The Defence of the Kingdom against Invasions.*

15 In the 17th century, the Senior Council Clerk was ex officio Muster Master General of England and Wales, which means that Waad still held this post. This is confirmed by a letter addressed to his wife, requesting the return of muster books to the council chest following William Waad's death in 1623.

16 House of Commons 1558-1603, p.560.

17 Dixon, p.161 – Norbrook House, Warwickshire, the home of John Grant married to Robert and Thomas Wintour's sister Dorothy.

CHAPTER NINE

POST PLOT TOWER – THE INTELLECTUALS

THE ARRIVAL OF THE Gunpowder Plotters at the Tower in November 1605 had made little difference to the comfort of the long-term prisoners. Sir Walter Ralegh, Lord Cobham and Lord Grey all had comfortable rooms, but when the Earl of Northumberland was sent to the Tower on November 27, things had to change. As the Earl was of much higher rank than the other prisoners he was entitled to the best accommodation, so Lord Grey was asked to move out of his quarters to make room for him. After two and half years in the Tower, Grey did not see why he should move for anybody, and saw this as a possible opportunity to gain his freedom. In numerous letters to Salisbury he pleaded for release. In the meantime, it was Waad who provided Northumberland with accommodation in the 'upper rooms' of his house on the site. Eventually, Grey agreed to move from his rooms, despite the fact that he felt 'he would die if he was denied his few comforts'.[1] The Earl of Northumberland, a man of intelligence and wealth, who possessed enormous estates mainly in the north, soon found fault with Grey's quarters which had been vacated for him. Even though they were the King's own rooms, Northumberland found them damp and stuffy, so he stayed in Waad's upper rooms until the Martin Tower could be prepared for him. Here the Earl set himself up in a suite of rooms, employed his own cook and other servants, dined off gold and silver plate and furnished his rooms with the finest hangings and carpets.

A nervous populace, and jumpy guards, gave rise to a number of incidences in the months following the Gunpowder Plot. Towards the end of 1605, Waad's attention was drawn to a ship of sixty to seventy tonnes, moored alongside the Tower Wharf for weeks that was reputed to be loaded with 100 barrels of gunpowder. Even though the Tower itself contained considerable stores of gunpowder,[2] there were heightened fears when it was learned that the ship was destined for Spain. Another scare on March 22, 1606, concerned a rumour that King James had been killed along with other noblemen who had attempted to defend him. Waad immediately raised the bridge, confiscated all keys belonging to inferior officers and put a guard on all gates. Then he confined his prisoners to their quarters and primed the Tower guns for action. Rumours circulating indicated that the murderers were English Jesuits, Spaniards and Frenchmen, or even Scotsmen wearing women's apparel.[3] The whole thing was a pack of lies, but it does indicate the apprehension of a nation in shock. After the rumours were proven to be completely false, James was able to welcome his brother-in-law for a State Visit in the summer. King Christian of Denmark arrived with King James and Prince Henry at the Tower as part of his visit to London where he 'surveyed all the offices and munitions'. He was given a general tour and then ascended the White Tower where he discharged a piece of ordnance. During this visit, Waad once again had problems with the Lord Mayor who intended to arrive 'with his sword up' at the outer gates of the Tower to receive King James and the King of Denmark. Waad complained that 'this royal castle renowned in all christendom is so hemmed in by the City as there is no scope at all without [outside] the gates'. The Mayor was told not to come closer to the Tower than the end of Tower Street. After this almost comic interlude, the guests and their chief attendants were treated to a royal banquet by Sir William.[4]

The post plot investigations rumbled on and even Thomas Phelippes, the one time government spy, forger and cryptographer who had been Walsingham's Chief of Operations, was still under suspicion and was re-arrested in February 1606, though he had denied any connection with Father Garnet or the Gunpowder Plot. Waad of course had worked with Phelippes, and knew him well when they had both worked for Walsingham. In fact, after Walsingham died he had begged Waad to recommend him to Salisbury for a job in intelligence.[5] He gave a full account to Waad and asked the King's pardon. The cryptographer claimed that his link with Father Owen was a government strategem organised in Queen Elizabeth's time, and tried to explain away the presents he had received from Spain. He insisted that he had been given no money by Father Baldwin and claimed that his troubles had been caused by malice.[6] Neither Salisbury nor Waad seemed willing to let go of this particular aspect of the plot, as both were terriers. They wanted Hugh Owen, Sir William Stanley and William Baldwin extradited from the continent. Owen moved to Spain and Stanley remained at liberty, but Baldwin, the priest from Cornwall, was arrested on his way to Rome in 1610. From Dusseldorf, he was brought to the Tower in fetters, 'trussed up like a lion'.[7] Waad received him courteously and ensured that he lacked nothing. Despite no charges being brought against him, he was kept there for another eight years.

The Earl of Northumberland was brought before the Star Chamber on June 27, 1606, and although most of the evidence against him was circumstantial, the authorities were determined to make an example of him, so he faced trial for three contempts.[8] He was found guilty. His sentence was 'imprisonment at the king's pleasure', loss of all public offices and a huge fine. A man who could pay a fine of £30,000 for his very minor part as the Catholic figurehead in the Gunpowder Plot could easily afford to pay Waad £100 annually for the inconvenience he was causing to the routine of the Tower. He also built himself a bowling alley with a canvas roof, and had new windows pierced to bring in more light to his laboratory.[9]

Sir William now found himself presiding over prisoners who were great men and intellectuals, and the Tower became a place of scholarship and scientific experiments. Grey spent much of his time in correspondence. Cobham had a huge library and read and translated from the classics. Ralegh conducted scientific experiments trying to extract the salt from seawater, made cordials and wrote his *'History of the World'*. Northumberland's interests were in the realm of astrology and philosophy. He also made medicines and potions, and his mathematical friends would gather round for discussions with him. Waad may well be criticised for the treatment of his prisoners but his tolerance of these quirky individuals allowed a flowering of philosophical thought and discovery never to be equalled again in the history of the Tower.

In 1608 the Plague revisited the Tower. Waad had learnt that in the past, when the Plague was severe, previous Lieutenants had removed important prisoners from the Tower to their own homes until the fear had subsided. He knew that his duty was to guard and protect his charges, but 'to leave the disposing of them for liberty or restraint to His Majesty and to meddle no further'. However, he realised that both he and they were in great danger of being infected and sought Salisbury's advice on what to do with his charges. He used this occasion to mention once again the encroachments of tenements both inside and outside the walls of the Tower. Waad had complained every year about the many 'base tenements' which were built around the Bulwark, outside the gate and along the ditch side, because in times of plague these hovels seemed to be first to be infected. In previous plague-years all the inhabitants of these buildings had died, but at Waad pointed out, 'the Gentleman Porter, who receives benefit by these base tenements' was absent after midsummer so that the danger threatened not him, but those 'whose attendance is tied to this place, as his ought to be'. When Waad's own personal porter, a youth from Jersey, showed symptoms of illness he placed the lad in a remote part of the Tower. The porter seemed to recover, but Waad was obviously concerned about the lad's welfare because he sent him into the country 'to a house of mine to avoid suspicion of danger'. As Waad pointed out to Salisbury, they were 'besieged' and could not leave the Tower in safety except by water, and even then they had to pass the infected houses.[10] Waad had inherited a Tower surrounded by tenements and slums, and there was little he could do about it except complain to the authorities.

The Lieutenant had overall control, not just of the Tower, but also the Royal Mint and Armoury which formed a bustling community employing labourers, warders, servants, craftsmen, storekeepers, mint-workers and armourers. It was a busy workshop as well as being the storehouse of the nation's wealth in coins and jewels and all the records of government. Even before Waad's time, it had become a tourist attraction as we learn when Paul Hentzner, a German traveller, had been shown round in 1597. He had to leave his sword at the gatehouse, before being allowed in, and then was shown some of the treasures – over a hundred pieces of 'arras' (carpets) belonging to the Crown, made of gold, silver and silk, plus saddles, bed furniture, canopies and royal dresses. In the armoury he was shown spears, shields, halberds, lances and the body armour of Henry VIII, which is still on display at the Tower today. He was also shown cannon, one of which could fire seven balls at a time, as well as simple crossbows, bows and arrows. The Menagerie was of great interest to tourists, and it was here, in September 1607, that a further lion cub was born.[11]

Waad's difficulties with the Lord Mayor continued over their various responsibilities at the Tower, and began to impinge on Waad's 'ancient privilege' of the right to 'bombards'* of wine which was received as a traditional payment to the Lieutenant of the Tower from London merchants. The merchants, who began to take sides with the Mayor, not only refused to give him the wine but one actually beat up Waad's servant who was collecting the duty and stole the bottles back from him. Unhappy about not receiving his share, Waad tried to resolve the matter himself, but in the end decided to leave it to the due process of the law.[12]

The subject of money was always close to Waad's heart, and unlike his predecessor who made a serious loss during his brief time as Lieutenant, Waad was concerned to receive what was due to him. The King gave instructions to the Exchequer to produce a warrant for £8 weekly to Waad for the maintenance of Lord Thomas Grey of Wilton, plus £100 yearly for 'physic, apparel and other necessaries' which was the same as for Lord Cobham.[13] During the time of King James the allowance for comestibles, wine and fuel for the meals of an imprisoned earl, including payments for gaolers and the Lieutenant's servants in attendance on him, was estimated at £12 15s.0d. per week. When payments were late arriving, Waad wrote to Salisbury asking to be paid for the diet of prisoners. He pointed out that previous Lieutenants were paid at the end of each quarter, whereas he had not been paid for a whole half-year which meant that he was obliged to use his own money to finance the run-

---

* Bombard – large leather vessel containing liquor (in this case wine).

ning-costs of the Tower, which was consuming his 'weak estate'.[14] Waad was equally concerned to collect the dues of prisoners payable to the Tower. When Sir Everard Digby was arrested, he possessed two trunks in Aldersgate Street in which he had £100 in gold and £50 in white money. Waad asked permission to take £50 from these trunks to provide Digby with food and bedding. The Sheriff of Warwickshire had apparently already helped himself to £400.[15]

Long after the Plot enquiries had run their course, there were still plenty of problems to keep Waad busy at the Tower, some of them as a consequence of the Gunpowder Plot. Several people wanted to buy leases of property within the Tower precincts, like Thomas Passe, the Master Smith, who went over Sir William's head and wrote direct to the Privy Council asking them to consider his status in the Tower. Passe had been refused admission to the forge and the house adjoining it, because they were said not to belong to him but to the Smith of the Mint. Thomas felt that he was entitled to this property. In the past, the house next door to the Lieutenant's lodgings had been occupied by the Master Smith of the Office of the Ordinance, but because of heightened fear of explosions the Smith's residence had been moved to another part of the Tower. William Hubbock, the Tower Chaplain, was claiming residence. As there had been considerable use for his services during the Plot interrogations, no doubt he felt that he had earned a permanent place there. There were the usual administrative affairs to handle, like appointing warders and dealing with leave of absence. Waad often left the Tower for as much as a month at a time and needed to make sure that his assistants, Sir Roger Dallison, Sir John Kay and Edward Forcett, were available to cover for him.[16] He dealt with the receiving of prisoners such as priests and recusants, arranged money for wages and the diet of his prisoners, and sent reports of his examination of prisoners to the Privy Council, particularly on the 'traitorous Jesuits'. At this point, William was still trying to stem the flow of 'pestiferous' books being imported from the Continent. In the evenings, he entertained for dinner those prisoners who had permission to eat with him. In 1607 it was Sir Thomas Sherley the younger, a privateer, or pirate, who had been in and out prison, both here and abroad. On this occasion, he was in gaol for trying to interfere with the operations of the Levant Company.[17] Later, it was the Earl of Northumberland and Father Garnet who ate with him and his family in his private quarters.

Sir William had enjoyed the power and privileges of his office for nearly eight years now, but things were about to change and he was destined to leave the Tower before many of his charges. Lord Grey died in the Tower in 1614. Cobham was released in 1617 and died starving and penniless in 1619. Ralegh had a stroke in his mid-fifties in the spring of 1606. He was released on March 19, 1616 to enter upon his final journey to find Eldorado, but did not set sail until 1617 and when his mission failed, he was returned to the Tower and executed on October 29, 1618, at Westminster.[18] The Earl of Northumberland was imprisoned indefinitely in the Tower where he continued to live magnificently despite his incarceration. He remained there until 1621, when his son-in-law Lord Hay obtained his release.[19]

Notes

1 HMC XVIII, Grey to Salisbury, p.598.

2 ibid p.548.

3 Nichols, *Progresses* Vol. II, p.39.

4 ibid July 28, 1606, p.211.

5 CSP Domestic 1598-1601, April 1600.

6 HMC XIX, p.303.

7 CSP Venetian, Oct. 21, 1610, Venetian Ambassador in England to Doge.

8 Firstly, he had positioned himself as head of Catholics in England; secondly, he had made Thomas Percy, a known 'jesuited recusant', a gentlemen pensioner, but failed to ensure he had been sworn in; thirdly, he had tried to recover his rents from Percy in the north without ordering Percy's apprehension. Nicholls, Mark, *Investigating Gunpowder Plot*, pp. 186-7.

9 HMC XVII, Waad to Salisbury, Nov. 26, 1605, p.514, and Lacy Robert, *Sir Walter Raleigh*, p.319.

10 HMC XX, Sep. 1608.

11 ibid XIX, p.258.

12 ibid XVIII, p.120.

13 ibid XIX, p.380.

14 ibid p.81.

15 ibid XVII, p.502.

16 CSP Domestic James I, July 6, 1608, p.446 and July 18, 1610, p.624.

17 HMC XIX, p.280: DNB Vol.50, p.317.

18 Oxford DNB on-line version, Sir Walter Ralegh.
19 Batho, *Wizard Earl* pp 344-7; Fraser, p.276.

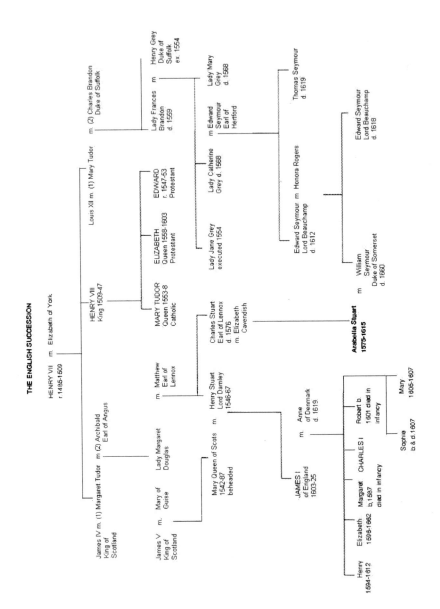

THE ENGLISH SUCCESSION

HENRY VII   m.   Elizabeth of York
r 1485-1509

James IV m. (1) Margaret Tudor m (2) Archibald
King of   Earl of Angus
Scotland

Louis XII m. (1) Mary Tudor   m.   (2) Charles Brandon
                                                         Duke of Suffolk

HENRY VIII
King 1509-47

James V   m.   Mary of   Lady Margaret
King of   Guise   Douglas
Scotland

m. Matthew
    Earl of
    Lennox

MARY TUDOR   ELIZABETH   EDWARD
Queen 1553-8   Queen 1558-1603 r. 1547-53
Catholic   Protestant   Protestant

Lady Frances   m   Henry Grey
Brandon   Duke of
d. 1559   Suffolk
                    ex. 1554

Mary Queen of Scots   m.
1542-87
beheaded

Henry Stuart
Lord Darnley
1546-67

Charles Stuart
Earl of Lennox
d. 1576
m. Elizabeth
Cavendish

Lady Jane Grey   Lady Catherine
executed 1554   Grey d. 1568

m Edward
  Seymour
  Earl of
  Hertford

Lady Mary
Grey
d. 1568

JAMES I   m.   Anne
of England   of Denmark
1603-25   d. 1619

Arabella Stuart
1575-1615

Edward Seymour m Honora Rogers
Lord Beauchamp
d. 1612

Thomas Seymour
d. 1619

m   William
            Seymour
            Duke of Somerset
            d. 1660

Edward Seymour
Lord Beauchamp
d. 1618

Henry   Elizabeth   Margaret   CHARLES I   Robert b
1594-1612   1596-1662   b. 1597   1601 died in
                             died in infancy   infancy

Mary
1605-1607

Sophie
b & d. 1607

94

CHAPTER TEN

DISGRACE
ARABELLA'S JEWELS AND THE
OVERBURY INCIDENT

LIFE IN THE TOWER, despite its challenges and frustrations, had been a satisfying and exciting one, but after six years in the post Waad's problems increased. In 1611 his young son died, to be followed in 1612 by the death of his patron, Salisbury, and in 1613 he was dismissed from his post as Lieutenant of the Tower.[1]

For some years Waad had pinned his hopes upon his young heir, Armigel, who died while the family were living at the Tower. For a sixty-five-year-old man to lose his seven-year-old heir must have been a shattering blow. In his copy of Erebus' 'Calendar' William describes Armigel as 'a child of great wit, modesty, piety and discretion above his age'.[2] He was taken from the Tower to be buried at Hampstead, with his grandfather namesake, in the chancel of the parish church near the main family home at Belsize. At least Sir William was fortunate in having one other son who was to become his heir. This was three-year-old James, named after the King who had agreed to be his godfather.

The death of Robert Cecil, the 1st Earl of Salisbury, in 1612, severed the Waad links with the Cecil family that had existed for so many years. As the Cecils rose to greatness so the Waad family had prospered. As Lord Burghley and Salisbury became the foremost men of their time so Armigel and Sir William increased their power and authority. Though always in the shadow of their masters they were nevertheless diplomats in their own right and there was a rumour that, despite his age, Sir William might step into Salisbury's shoes to become Secretary when he died, but this was not to be.[3]

Lord William Burghley, Salisbury's father, had been visited on his deathbed by Queen Elizabeth who had tended and even fed him, but the death of Salisbury had little real effect on the power or feelings of King James. By the end of 1611, Salisbury was seriously ill, and in spring of the following year he decided to take the waters in Bath for his health. He died at Marlborough on May 24, 1612 on his return journey, no doubt to the satisfaction of his enemies Rochester and Northampton who now came into their own.[4] As Waad then lacked the necessary support at Court, he was soon dismissed from his post on a trumped up charge. The official reasons given were Lady Arabella Stuart's complaint that Waad had embezzled some of her jewels, and that he was slack in allowing too much freedom to some of his prisoners, but the underlying reason was that he was considered to be too efficient a guardian of his charges in the Tower.[5]

Lady Arabella Stuart was a sad figure. Although she was the cousin of James I, and a niece of Mary, Queen of Scots, for much of her life she was kept a virtual prisoner. In her early years she spent a good deal of time with her grandmother, the Countess of Shrewsbury, Bess of Hardwick, who was very fond of her, but as Arabella grew older she was kept virtually under house-arrest in her own household, only rarely being given permission to attend Court. Because of her royal connections, she was sometimes used as a figurehead for plots against the monarchy. In most cases she was perfectly innocent but her name was linked to the Bye and Main plots of 1603. Although there were Spanish plots to abduct and use her as a possible new sovereign when James was removed from the throne, she was allowed back at Court after Ralegh's trial, though she does not appear to have enjoyed Court life and was always impecunious. James had enough children of his own to ensure the succession, but distrusted her, and insisted that she should not marry without his permission. However, at the end of 1609, Arabella fell in love with, and secretly married William Seymour who was twelve years her junior. Though they did not live together, after seventeen days of marriage Seymour was observed on a number of occasions visiting Arabella's apartment. He was arrested, confessed, and was sent to the Tower. A warrant was then issued for Arabella's arrest.

She was kept under detention in Sir Thomas Parry's house from where she frequently wrote to Seymour and sent pleading letters to the Council and the Queen.

As Waad's prisoner in the Tower, Seymour complained of rheumatism caused by the dampness of his lodging in St. Thomas' Tower above Traitor's Gate, and was soon allowed to move to better quarters and have two servants of his own. But when the King heard that the two lovers were openly corresponding with each other, he ordered that Arabella be moved even further away into the custody of the Bishop of Durham. On her journey northwards, she had only reached Barnet in Hertfordshire when she became ill and her guards sought advice about moving her further. Here she planned her escape to coincide with William Seymour's decision to escape from the Tower. If the timing had not gone slightly awry the dramatic escape of the two lovers seeking happiness abroad could so easily have happened. Arabella, disguised as a man, was taken to London by her servants and was rowed out from Blackwall to meet a French ship which would take her to the continent.[6] All went well for her and she finally boarded the French barque to await her husband's arrival. Seymour's escape from the Tower was brilliant, but delayed. He disguised himself as a humble workman and simply walked out behind a cart as it left the Tower precincts. When Waad heard that one of his most important prisoners had escaped, he was incandescent and ordered Seymour's valet, called Batten, to be flung into a dungeon before he galloped to Greenwich to break the unwelcome news to the King. The French captain refused to wait in the Thames estuary any longer for Seymour and sailed for Calais. The response of the English authorities was so prompt that Arabella's ship was chased across the Channel and stopped before it could land. Arabella was brought back, arrested and taken immediately to the Tower. In the meantime, Seymour had arrived at Ostende in a desperate attempt to discover the whereabouts of Arabella. He never saw her again. Waad, having lost the husband, now took custody of the wife. She remained in the Tower and was to die there in 1615; a forty-year-old disappointed, and by all accounts, deranged princess. Though most of her wealth was seized when she was arrested, and the money used to pay for the cost of following and detaining her, she must have had a few precious stones in her possession on entering the Tower because Ralegh was later known to possess some of these. In May 1613, only a year after his protector Salisbury had died, a warrant was issued for the arrest of Sir William Waad, who it was claimed, had seized Seymour's goods when he fled from the Tower. Northampton sent his agent to Waad's 'mansion at Charing Cross'[7] to bring in his prisoner. Sir William was also charged with embezzling some of Arabella's jewels. Waad's wife was implicated too and his daughter was actually imprisoned.[8] However, this was only the beginning of the Lieutenant's problems.

Sir William Waad's dismissal probably had nothing to do with Arabella Stuart's jewels. This was simply used as an excuse to oust him from the position Lieutenant of the Tower, because he was far too diligent in guarding his prisoners and was unlikely to be seduced by bribery. The catalyst for this event was almost certainly the arrival of Sir Thomas Overbury at the Tower only two or three weeks before Waad was dismissed. But Sir William had received prior notice of his own discharge through Mrs. Anne Horne, a servant of Frances the Countess of Essex who had previously worked for Lady Waad. Mrs. Horne admitted that as she could never please her new mistress, Lady Frances, she had decided to warn the Waads whom she admired. She later told Waad that her Lord (Somerset) was 'never gladder than when he heard that Overbury was dead.'[9]

The plan to poison Sir Thomas Overbury could never have succeeded with Waad in office, so powerful political forces were used to remove him. Overbury had been the friend and adviser of royal favourite Robert Carr, Earl of Somerset. The King, who took an unnatural pleasure in the body of Carr, especially his legs, experienced 'more delight in his company and conversation than in any man's living'. But as well as pleasing the King, Carr became the object of desire of Frances Howard, daughter of Thomas Howard, Earl of Suffolk and his wife Katherine Rich (née Knevet.)* Frances was now the wife of Robert Devereux, the 3rd Earl of Essex, whom she

---

* Sir Thomas Knyvett, keeper of the palace at the time of gunpowder plot, was Suffolk's brother-in-law.

had come to hate.* At first Overbury helped Robert and Frances in their illicit affair, but when Overbury saw the real nature of Frances below her surface beauty, he warned Carr that she was not good enough for him. This caused the two friends to became bitter enemies. Frances tried to divorce her husband, Essex, by claiming that the marriage was unconsummated, so that she might marry Robert Carr. To get rid of her enemy, she persuaded King James to send Overbury to Russia as ambassador. James resented Overbury's influence over his favourite, Carr, so he was not difficult to convince. When Overbury refused to accept the post he was placed in the Tower where, unbeknown to James, Frances planned to have him poisoned.[10]

In order to expedite this plan, it was necessary to replace Sir William Waad's tight regime with a more relaxed one. Sir Gervais Elwys of Lincolnshire was her preferred choice for the task of Lieutenant of the Tower. Elwys was a gambler who had once played the part of the Lord of Misrule at the Inns of Court Christmas festivities – a part he was required to play in earnest at the Tower. As was common practice at the time, Elwys had to pay £2,000 for the privilege of office, of which £1,400 went to the Earl of Northampton and £300 to Monson, who was the Master of the Armoury in the Tower, and a friend of Elwys. As a result of this bribery and corruption, the gaoler appointed by Waad to guard Overbury was replaced by Richard Weston, a servant of Frances and Carr, making their sinister task easier. Waad was furious when he was blamed for 'using too much favour to Overbury and suffering him to lie in my lodging'. Naturally he felt aggrieved. Overbury was only being held in custody, so Waad felt that he had the power to treat him in a considerate manner; especially as Waad's wife and children were away from the Tower lodgings at that time. After a period of eight years successful governorship, Waad was angry that his so-called 'loose government and liberty given to the prisoners' was criticised. He protested that he had refused all access to Overbury, 'even to

---

* Robert Devereaux, 3rd Earl of Essex was the son of Robert Devereaux, 2nd Earl of Essex, who had been Queen Elizabeth's favourite during her latter years. The 2nd Earl was executed in 1601 for his part in the Essex Rebellion.

the Earl of Somerset's servants,' because of course, Waad was a stickler for rules and regulations, whereas Elwys, called 'a creature of the Lord Chamberlain' was more complacent. Therefore, it was not long before 'liberty was given to the condemned men as they walked and talked together, played at cards and other pastimes, which liberty never before was seen there'.[11]

Overbury seems to have been aware that there were plans afoot to dispose of him because he observed that the wife of Warder Langton became very ill after consuming some broth intended for him.[12] Even though Overbury was kept away from the other prisoners, it still took four months of persistence before various poisons, smuggled into the Tower in tarts and glass phials, finally succeeded in killing him. Elwys may have protected Overbury for a time, and intercepted the poisoned wines, tarts and jellies destined for him, but he could not prevent the determined efforts of others to kill him. Frances finally offered £20 to an apothecary's apprentice, William Reeve, to kill Overbury on September 14, 1613 by injecting into his body an enema poisoned with sublimate of mercury. The murder was hushed up for a time with Overbury's death being attributed to natural causes, although it is hard to believe that his stinking corpse, reputedly covered in sores, did not attract some suspicion.[13] Carr and the now divorced Frances were married, but when William Reeve fell seriously ill at Flushing he confessed to his part in Overbury's murder. This, and the persistent rumours of foul play, meant that a court case was inevitable. Frances received no support from her parents at this time who had fled to their house at Audley End[14] 'for shame at the arraignment'.[15] Carr and Frances were sentenced to death, but were later pardoned by the King.[16]

Waad's resentment at being expelled from office appears to be thoroughly justified, but the blow to Sir William's pride was somewhat assuaged in the eleventh year of James's reign when the King gave out a number of free gifts. Waad was given £500 'for reliquishing a grant of £2,000 out of recusants'. He also decided to resign his lifetime patent as Clerk of the Privy Council, in August 1613, after thirty years in the office. He sold his post as Clerk of the Privy Council to Mr. Cottington for £400.[17] It must have given Waad secret pleasure to see the mess that his successor got himself into over the death of Overbury, especially when Elwes was brought to trial, condemned and executed on November 20, 1615. Only then was Waad was able to tell his side of the story in the Overbury affair and justify his actions in the period before his dismissal.[18]

However, there was a distinct air of scandal surrounding Waad's departure, partly occasioned by the naivity of Waad's own daughter who seems to have been trying to assist Lady Arabella to escape. She provided Arabella with a key, and a wax imprint was made from it to enable a duplicate key to be cast. Instead of using it herself, Arabella asked Thomas Erskine, Viscount Fenton,* to take it directly to the King – no doubt as proof of Waad's inefficiency. The King certainly found 'just cause' to remove Waad. In a letter to the Earl of Marr, who was one of King James's close associates, Viscount Fenton told his friend that he suspected something important was going on. It does sound as if this was a concerted effort to remove Waad because Fenton suggested that Lord Grey was 'not altogether innocent'. Several women were arrested, including Mrs. Pairpoint, Lady Arabella's faithful servant, as well as Sir William Waad's own daughter. In fact, his daughter was actually imprisoned for a while for her complicity in making the duplicate key.[19] Fenton wrote, 'my old master Sir William Waad is removed out of the Tower by the device of the Lady Arabella and his own daughter. I dare not speak particulars by writing, tho the poor knight's indiscretion was the chiefest cause of his discharge'.[20] Was Waad set-up by the Howard family to enable them to install their own man, Elwys, or was Arabella trying to punish Waad who had prevented her happiness by keeping her away from the man she loved? Either way, the result was the same.

When Sir William lost his job as Lieutenant the charge against him was embezzling Arabella's jewels, and his wife and daughter were also suspected. However, there can be little truth in these claims because when Arabella was arrested, although she had £868 and a parcel of gold and her jewels in her possession, these were taken from her to pay her debts and for the cost of her capture, so

---

*Viscount Fenton, Earl of Kellie, was a close friend of King James and had been educated with him. The Earl of Mar, John Erskine, was Viscount Fenton's cousin.

there could have been very little left when she arrived at the Tower. When her husband, William Seymour, managed to escape dressed as a workman, he left behind him valuable possessions which he had arranged to be placed in his rooms, but Waad had actually paid for many of these on Seymour's behalf. After Seymour's escape, Waad wrote to Salisbury giving a detailed list of Seymour's effects, and claimed the goods as his due in repayment of debts incurred by Seymour for medicine and tapestries.[21] Once on the continent, Seymour demanded that these goods be restored to him and tried to sue Sir William for the return of his possessions left in Waad's care. The Privy Council, however, refused to allow Waad to be sued until Seymour returned to the kingdom. They even threatened Samuel Smith, who was acting for Seymour, that if he continued with his legal action he would be 'restrained of his liberty and committed to prison'.[22] At least the Council showed some support for Sir William, despite his embarrassing departure from office.

Notes

1 CSP Domestic 1611-1618, p.185.
2 Rawlinson MSS, f.61 b3.
3 McClure, *Chamberlain's letters II*, p.355.
4 DNB on-line.
5 May 13, 1613, Wm. Waad discharged from Lieutenancy of the Tower on complaint of having embezzled the jewels of Lady Arabella.
6 CSP Domestic James I, Jun 5, 1611, p.39.
7 Dixon, p.467.
8 ibid Lake to Carleton, p.185.
9 CSP Domestic 1611-1618, May 19, 1613, and Dec. 4,1615.
10 In 1606 Frances Howard, niece of Lord Henry Howard, was a child bride to Robert Devereux, son of the Earl of Essex. They had to wait four years before living together as man and wife during which time she fell for Robert Carr. Overbury was sent to the Tower Apr. 21, CSP Domestic James I, p.181.
11 CSP Domestic James I, May 13, 1613, and HMC Marquess of Downshire Vol. 4, Sir J. Throckmorton to Wm. Trumbull, May 12, 1613.
12 CSP Domestic James I, Sep. 1615 and ibid Waad to Salisbury p.323.
13 Lindley, *Trials of Frances Howard*, p.146.
14 Thomas Howard began a colossal building project at Audley End House, Essex in 1603. When completed in 1616, it covered five acres and was probably the largest house in England in private hands.

15 DNB online; and Somerset, pp 14-15.
16 CSP Domestic, Sherburn to Carleton, May 27, 1616.
17 ibid Waad to Coke, Oct 31, 1615.
18 ibid p.198 Aug.23, 1613.
19 CSP Domestic, 1611-1618, Sep. 1615.
20 ibid p.185, Thomas Lake to Carlton, May 1613; HMC Earl of Marr &
    Kellie, p. 51/2, Viscount.Fenton to Earl of Marr, May 20, 1613; HMC MSS
    of Marquess of Downshire, Vol. IV, Samuel Calvert to Wm. Trumbull, June
    4, 1613.
21 CSP Domestic James I, Dec. 10, 1611, p.98.
22 APC, May, 1615.

CHAPTER ELEVEN

THE FINAL YEARS

ALTHOUGH WAAD HAD NOW lost his post as Lieutenant, and had resigned as Clerk to the Privy Council, the Council nevertheless recognised his experience as Muster-Master General and decided to appoint him as a local official for Middlesex. In July 1616 a letter was sent to the Commissioner of Musters in Middlesex, reminding them that although there was no Lieutenant of the County they had appointed Sir William as Commissioner for Musters, 'for as much as we have had a long experience of the discretion and sufficiency of Sir William Waad in these and such other public services'.[1] Even though Sir William may have been tainted by the Overbury Plot, and rumours of purloining some of Arabella's jewellery, this appointment indicates the faith that the Privy Council still had in him. Some individuals also appear to have respected Sir William. The Reverend Thomas Porter, of Hemnall in Norfolk, regarded him as worthy of trust, and wrote in fulsome Latin verse a dedication to him as distinguished soldier and friend, praising his virtue and expressing his certainty that his fame will be restored when King James realised the truth behind his loyalty as the previous Lieutenant of the Tower.

Indeed there was another, more compassionate side to Sir William's character that was not much in evidence during his time at the Tower. For some years both before, and long after, losing his post as Lieutenant of the Tower, William was responsible for writing to various county justices trying to obtain money for soldiers wounded in various wars. This appears to have been one of his responsibilities as Muster-Master General. Some had become deaf from the noise of cannon shot, others had lost the use of their eyes.[2] These men were often failed by their own county officials, so Waad intervened on their behalf and with the support of Privy Council, to obtain pensions for them. For years the Privy Council, with Waad as their agent, had been concerned about the reduced amount of money being levied by each county for the relief of maimed soldiers. In one instance the local authorities had refused to help wounded soldiers, using the relief fund instead to build a house of correction, to the fury of The Privy Council.[3] Waad also had to deal with requests for assistance from company captains whose pay was stopped when they returned to England for short periods from towns, like Brill, in the Low Countries.[*]

Waad's legal work continued throughout the time he was Lieutenant of the Tower and after he lost his post. He was a serious man who seems to have displayed ceaseless energy thoughout his long life. He is described by the antiquarian David Lloyd, as intelligent, a scholar, and 'grave in his life and manners' but 'pleasant in his carriage and complexion'. He was 'a man of constant toyl and industry, busie and quick equally, an enemy to the idle and slow undertaking, judging it a great weakness to stand staring the face of business'. We are told that he could not bear to be idle but immediately set to work on a new project when the present one was finished.[4] And these characteristics certainly explain his enormous capacity for work throughout his entire career, and especially during the hectic period of the Gunpowder Conspiracy.

In April 1613 he was a member of the Court of Sessions concerned with the price of bread and beer and the rates for servants' wages.[5] In the latter part of his retirement, Waad spent more time away from Belsize at Battles Hall, his farm in Essex, where he was busy rebuilding the house,[6] but his public work continued, officiating at the Quarter Sessions in Essex. In 1620 he sat with Lord Maynard, of Great Easton, Essex, when he dealt with the case of Edward Wymble of Chrishall for erecting a cottage on the Lord's waste. As if this wasn't crime enough, the man was also found to be keeping a house of bawdery there, as well as thieving from the customers 'to the annoyance of the inhabitants'. In what was probably one of his last attendances in 1622, Waad dealt with various cases

---

[*] Den Briel, Low Countries, or Nederland – (Holland).

of public disorder in his neighbouring village of Rickling.

After a lifetime of dealing with national problems, Waad was asked to assist in a local dispute just a few years before his death. John Person was an elderly man from Manuden's neighbouring parish of Farnham who had once been a stalwart of the church and a churchwarden in 1598. For some reason Person had stopped going to church and had been excommunicated by his vicar. But now this poor, old, blind and repentant man longed to return to the spiritual comfort of the church, but he was unable to pay the fine of twelve pence demanded by the churchwardens. A number of local people drew up a petition in his support. The local vicar, Mr. Symons, refused to give way unless he was presented with an official, sealed letter from other local vicars and Waad was asked to intervene. Waad appealed on his behalf and asked the vicar of Elsenham to write an official letter, duly sealed, which would encourage Symons to submit to the will of the parishioners.[7]

After his 'last great sickness' at Belsize, Waad spent much more time at Battles Hall, Manuden, and drew up his Will there in 1618. He made detailed provision for the burial of his body, whether he should die in London or at Battles. If in London, he wanted to be buried beside his young son and his own father, in the chancel at Hampstead, and if in Essex, in the area of the church where the family pew was positioned in Manuden church. His Will shows clearly that he had made some good friends in this part of the country, like Mr. Thomas Thompson from Berden, Essex and Mr. Maurice Parson of Pelham, Hertfordshire, and he seems to have been especially friendly with the vicar of Manuden, Israel Thornell. He was particularly grateful to his old friend and secretary, John Lorcason, to whom he bequeathed 'a pair of plate' with a value of £4 – he had already leased him a house in Hampstead. Waad regarded Lorcason as a very wise, honest and discreet gentleman. William appealed to these men and to the Clerk of the Privy Council, Mr. Cottington (Waad's replacement), as well as to the Secretary of State, Sir George Calvert, to assist in his son's upbringing in the event of his wife's death, particularly since he had been an honourable servant of the government for thirty years following his worthy father's loyal service.

The Waad memorial in St. Mary's Church, Manuden, Essex.

When Sir William died in October 1623, his friend, the vicar of Manuden, reported the event in the parish records as 'my loving and dear friend buried 21st October'. In his Will he had requested a burial, without solemnity of funeral charges, in the chapel on the north side of the church. No tomb or ledger stone exists; however, a memorial in Latin on the north wall of Manuden Church was erected. This was renovated by William de Vins Waad of Dunmow in the late 1800s. The following is a translation:

Sir William Waad, Knight, son of Armigild, Secretary to the Lady Elizabeth's Privy Council many years, sent once to the Emperor Rudolphus and to Philip of Spain, and to Henry III, King of France, thrice to Henry IV of France and Navarre, and once to Mary, Queen of Scotland, on various occasions

107

of the greatest importance. Commissary-General of England
and Superintendent of the Soldiery in Ireland, and also
Secretary to the Privy Council of our most serene Lord
King James, and Lieutenant of the London Tower eight years.
Afterwards living privately and religiously till his 77th year,
and died at his manor of Battailes-Wade in the county of Essex
on the 21st day of October, in the year of our Lord, 1623.

Below the Latin list of his various diplomatic appointments is
a piece of verse, in English, which likens his life to the 'Watch of
State.' The writer of the memorial uses the device of an Elizabethan
conceit to compare William to a clock, and to advise those who
would be perfect servants of the state to copy its accuracy and to
compare themselves with his example. The minutes of his life were
spent on religious thoughts; his hours spent doing good deeds. His
main thought was always the good of the kingdom and the safety of
its sovereign. Although ambitious, he could never be persuaded or
bribed to do evil and he died with a clear conscience. His zeal kept
him wound up like a coiled spring on earth, so that at his death, he
would be suddenly released and elevated straight to heaven.

YOV THAT HAVE PLACE AND CHARGE FROM PRINCES TRUST
WHOM HONORS MAYE MAKE THANKEFVLL NOT VNIVST
DRAWE NEARE AND SET YOVR CONSCIENCE AND YOVR CARE
BY THIS TRVE WATCH OF STATE WHOSE MINVTES WERE
RELIGIOUS THOVGHTS, WHOSE HOWERS HEAVENS SACRED FOODE
WHOSE HAND STILL POINTED TO THE KINGDOMS GOOD
AND SOVERAIGNES SAFTIE WHOM AMBITIONS KEY
NEVER WOOND VP GVILTINES BRIBE OR FEE
ZEALE ONLY AND A CONSCIENCE CLEAR AND EVEN
RAYSED HIM ON EARTH AND WOOND HIM VP TO HEAVEN

Thus ended the life of a trusted public servant who had served
two monarchs during an extremely complex period of English history. He had served his patron Sir Robert Cecil, Lord Salisbury, dutifully throughout the whole course of the Gunpowder Plot, and took
with him to the grave all the secrets he held about the true course
of these extraordinary events. Hated by many, loved by some, but
generally well-respected for his efficiency, determination and te-

nacity, Sir William was a product of his time. He believed implicitly in the rectitude of his actions. For him, Roman Catholicism was an anathema. The only true path to God was through the Protestant religion, so that any and all methods used in its preservation and perpetuation were justified. He never wavered from this course and died in the belief that he had served his country and his monarch to the best of his ability.

Notes

1 APC July 26, 1616.
2 APC May 5, 1613: Richard Sumner, gunner at Ostende in 1603, John Lee of Huntingdon and Peter Lutterell, a poor, old, blind soldier of London.
3 HMC Various Collections Vol.1, 1611: Thomas Hameling of Ringwood.
4 Lloyd's *Worthies*, p.489, edition 1766.
5 Middx. Co. Records, Old Series Vol. 1, Apr. 1, 1613, p.34.
6 Recent dendrochonological evidence on Battles Hall timbers show that the present house roof was constructed in 1607, when Sir William was still Lieutenant of the Tower. Waad rebuilt the house on an adjacent plot to the original moated site re-using some of the original materials from the first house. Source: Adrian Gibson, Vernacular Architecture Historian, and Dr. M.C. Bridge, Oxford Dendrochonology Laboratory 2005.
7 Geare J.G, *History of Farnham*

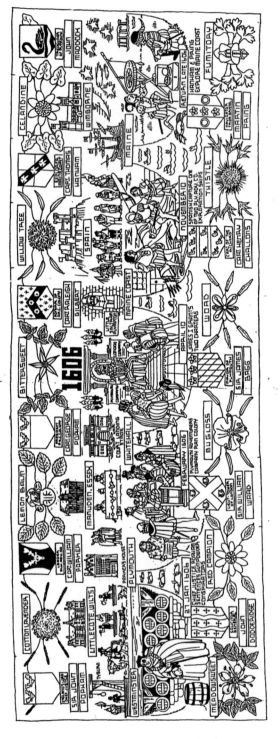

The 1605 Panel of the New World Tapestry, showing: a house in Manuden, Essex;
part of the coat of arms of Sir William Waad; and The Plymouth Adventurers Company.
Also, the coat of arms, and home, of Chief Justice Popham who sentenced the Gunpowder Conspirators.
The Tapestry can be viewed at:
The British Empire and Commonwealth Museum, Bristol.

110

POSTSCRIPT

By THE TIME OF his death William had built up considerable wealth and property. He was MP for Aldborough, Suffolk, and MP for Thetford, Norfolk during the parliament of November 1588 to March 1589. In May 1590 he had received a twenty-one year lease of St. John's Wood, adjacent to his house at Belsize in Hampstead and, three year's later, he was granted the annual rent* of several manors in Huntingdon, Nottingham, Buckingham, Kent, Derbyshire, Hertfordshire and Surrey for £40 a year. In 1601 he held the lucrative patent for making sulphur, brimstone and oil, inherited from his father, plus a part-share in an allum† patent which had also been granted to his father.[1] The patent for sulphur he fought hard to keep, even taking his late father's partner in this venture, William Herlle, to court in 1577, for arbitration over non-payment of funds.[2] This must have been an especially useful patent. After the King took over the monopoly he made £22,000 over two years. As MP for Preston, Lancashire, in 1601 he did sit in parliament on October 27, 1601, although judging by the records he never attended very often as a representative for any of his other seats after that date. From at least 1603, Waad was also a Commissioner for Causes Ecclesiastical.[3] More land came Sir William's way in 1604, when James I rewarded him for his work during Elizabeth's reign with the annual rents of manors and lands in the Duchy of Lancaster, valued at £60 a year plus manors in the counties of Leicester, Lancaster and York.[4] When Waad took over as Lieutenant of the Tower from Harvey in 1605, he also inherited his parliamentary seat of West Looe, now Port

* fee-farm – annual rent.
† potassium and its compounds.

Pigham, Cornwall.[5] In October 1605 he became Burgess of Bere Alston, Devon, as well.[6] His role as Muster-Master General was another profitable post, as the county muster-masters were obliged to pay him a share of the fines from defaulters and those excused from musters.[7]

Although not an adventurer like his father, Sir William had taken some steps towards emulating Armigel when he became a member of the Council for Virginia in 1607, and Member of the Council for the Virginia Company in 1609. Two companies were formed to pursue commercial interests in Virginia: The Plymouth Company, to exploit North Virginia which was primarily composed of Plymouth men,[8] and The Virginia Company of London, comprised of London men. These were commercial trading companies that had been chartered by King James I, in April 1606, with the objective of colonising the east coast of North America between latitudes 34° and 41° N. Ralegh, who had experience of Virginia after his ill-fated attempts to colonise there in the 1580s at a personal cost of over £40,000, wrote a paper for the council giving his advice on how to settle colonies in Virginia and, based on this, in December 1606 three ships set sail with 120 colonists. Waad and others bought Bermuda from the Virginia Company on November 25, 1612 for £2,000 and resigned the islands to the Crown in November 23, 1614. The islands had been obtained by Sir George Somers who was shipwrecked on the Bermudas in 1610 and claimed the islands for the Crown, naming them the Somers Islands.[9]

Word must have got round that Sir William was now a rich man, because in June 1608 William's house at Belsize was broken into and silver plate worth 30 shillings was stolen. The culprit, Yeoman William Dean, was arrested, held in prison, and charged after confessing. When he was tried in September, he pleaded benefit of clergy and was branded with a letter 'T' before being set free.[10] This privilege, once granted only to the clergy, had gradually been extended to include anyone who could prove his status and intelligence by reading a few verses from the Bible in court.

Some of Waad's wealth was willed to him by his father or acquired through his two advantageous marriages. In his Will he specifically refers to his major properties – the manor house and land of Battles, and the neighbouring estate of Peyton Hall, in Manuden, Essex. He also refers generally to his properties in the County of Middlesex, in the City of London, in Yorkshire, Lancashire and elsewhere in the realm of England.

James, his only male heir, who would have been about ten years old when William drew up his Will, was to receive the bulk of the property, including the leases of Belsize and St. John's Wood. William's wife, Anne, was well provided for and was left money for James' education as he was still a minor. This was to be increased to £100 a year when he turned fifteen years, to pay for his studies at University or the Inns of Court. William demonstrates his concern for all his children growing up in a troubled world, but most of the Will concerns the divisions of his property in the event of his only son's death. William wanted James to be brought up in a Christian manner and to be groomed for a profession. All his other children, eight daughters, are mentioned in the Will but they are only able to inherit if James dies before the age of twenty-one. Though William was in his seventies, most of his children were still young. He did live long enough to see some of them married: Abigail married John Whorwood in 1613 and Alyce married Philip Cage of Hormead, Hertfordshire on December 6, 1621 at Stocking Pelham Church, probably the last important family event before William's death. One has to wonder what William would have thought of Arminiagildea, who married into a branch of the Catholic Mordaunt family of Thunderley, Wimbish, in Essex, in 1629. Then there was Dorothea, who was probably unmarried, and Anne who was infirm and for whom money was left for her special care. Mary and Elizabeth were both to marry later in life. Mary was William's youngest daughter and became the second wife of John Holgate of Saffron Walden. Elizabeth married Edmund Lenthall, the nephew of the Speaker of the House of Commons, and descendents of this marriage still live in the Manuden area. William's daughter Jane, died unmarried at Southwark, in 1633, though all her writings were kept in a closet at Battles. She left small sums of money to her mother, brother and each of her sisters.[11]

Most of William's accumulated land went to James. This comprised the Manors of Battles and Peyton in Manuden, the house at

Charing Cross, a Parsonage and Glebe land at Hornchurch leased from New College, Oxford, and property leased from the Bishop and Chapter of London, in St. Martin's Lane, Strand. William refers to land at Hampstead, his property in Moor Lane, and houses and tenements in Greater St. Bartholomew, and his property in Whitechapel. He also left James land at Islington and Waltham Holy Cross. James entered Grays Inn on February 17, 1621. He did reach his majority to become a wealthy young man; nevertheless only eleven years after his father's death he was borrowing money and the family fortunes begin to decline.

If James did not reach twenty-one years, or have any children, then William wanted the properties divided up between his remaining children after the death of his wife. Battles Manor was to go to his daughter Abigail Whorwood, and Armeniagilda would inherit Peyton Hall, Manuden. Alyce was to receive leases of St. John's Wood and Hampstead, Jane the property in Moor Lane, Dorothea his houses in Great St. Bartholemews, Elizabeth his house and lands in Charing Cross and Mary his house and lands in Whitechapel. William's wife, Anne, to whom he refers with fondness in his Will, is left an income, the stuff, hangings and plate in his Charing Cross house and the choice of any other furnishings from a leased Parsonage at Hornchurch. She inherited the lease of a property in St. Martin's Lane, the Strand, and Sir William stipulated that she should be able to live at Belsize until their son, James, became twenty-one. These provisions were very sensible as Anne was to survive her husband by twenty-two years. Anne later married Thomas Bushell, who is recorded as being a servant of Francis Bacon.* No doubt Anne had met Thomas on the occasions when she and her husband met socially with Francis, as he was one of William's colleagues.[12]

James had two children, William, born in 1645, who married Anne Barlee, daughter of Haynes Barlee of Clavering, and Anne, born in 1651, who married Sir Edward Baesh of Stansted Abbots, Hertfordshire. William was murdered in July 1677 close to his home at Battles Hall, Manuden, as a result of a dispute over a gam-

---

* probably his secretary.

114

bling debt. Both William's children died young. His son William was born in 1665 and died in 1685, and his daughter Anne died in 1691 from smallpox. There is no record of any surviving issue from either of these children.

Belsize House no longer exists. It was entirely rebuilt in the reign of Charles II and demolished in 1852. The house is believed to have faced south-east over a brick-paved courtyard. It was situated near to the entrance of Hampstead village, and originally comprised 232 acres of parkland and meadow, bounded by a high stone wall on the south west dividing it from the forest of what is now St. John's Wood. Today, St. Peter's Church stands approximately on the site of the mansion, and the carriage-drive from the lodge to the house, along which Sir William and his father once rode, was from Haverstock Hill between the trees of Belsize Avenue.[13] Abigail Whorwood, who was probably William's oldest surviving child, was buried in Hampstead with her father and grandfather.[14] But sadly no record of the Waad family exists in Belsize or Hampstead following the demolition of Hampstead Church and all its monuments.

Lady Anne appears to have continued to live in the house for some years after her husband's death. The property eventually passed to John Holgate in about 1649 after the death of Anne in 1645. John was her daughter Mary's husband from Saffron Walden, Essex. The Holgate family are interred inside St. Mary's Church Saffron Walden. Several members of William Waad's family married locally and lived within the borders of Essex and Hertfordshire for many years following his death.

WAAD FAMILY TREE

(1) Alice Marbury = Armigell – Clk of PC. = (2) Alice Patten of Newington, Middx.
    widow of Bradley   Henry VIII & Edw. VI, JP Middx   Widow of Thos Searle, Essex
                b. 1511   bur. Hamstead
                d. 20 Jun. 1568 bur. Hampstead

Wm. Lt. of Tower   Thomas = Gertrude Pope   Margaret= Robert Jones   Anne   Joyce   Elizabeth
& Clk of PC, Eliz. I   d. 1594 bur St. Michael's   Clk Privy Seal
b. c. 1546   Basinghall, London
bur. Oct. 1623 Manuden

(1) **Ann** dau of Owen Waller   (2) **Anne** dau of Sir Humphrey Browne
& Emma Jurden, /Carter of Middx   b. c.1563/4   Remarried Thomas Bushell
b. c.1571 d. 1589   bur. Jun 22, 1643 Manuden   his obit 1660 Westminster Abbey

Armygild ?   Armigel   James. =   Frances Eltonhead   Abigail   =   John Whorwood
        Bapt. Sep.11   b. 1620   remarried   bap Jan 21,1597   of Compton, Staffs.
        1604 Hamps.   d 1659   Sir Jos. Douglas   bur. Hampstead
        d. 1611 Tower   in 1661   Dec 30, 1642

    William = Anne Barlee   Anne = Sir Edward Baesh
    b.1645   dau Haynes Barlee   b. 1651   of Stanstead Abbots
Murdered in Manuden   Clavering, Essex   Herts.
Jul. 16, 1677

William   Anne
b.1665   b. 1671 & d. 1691
d. 1685   of smallpox

    <u>no issue</u>

Armeniagilda = Charles Mordaunt   Alice = 2nd wife of Philip Cage   Jane   Elizabeth = Edmund Lenthall
b. c.1620   of Thunderley Essex   of Hormead   b. ?   bap 1607   nephew of Speaker
        Apr. 8, 1628   m. Stocking Pelham   d. 1633   Hampstead   of the House
                Herts. Dec.6, 1621
    Charles bur. Jan.19 1642
    In Manuden   William   Abigail
                Anthony   Elizabeth
                Thomas   Mary

Dorothea   Anne   Mary = 2nd wife John Holgate
        'infirm'   Bur.   of Saffron Walden, Essex
            S/Walden   m. Jan 28,1635

        Armigel bap. 1638
        Robert died young
        Ann m. James Monteith of Greenwich, Scotland

116

Notes

1 Cal. of Patent Rolls Elizabeth Vol. VII, June 8, 1577.

2 APC 1577.

3 HMC XV, p.223/4.

4 Cal. & Index of Patent Rolls, 31-37 Elizabeth, p.29, & 24; Mort Commons, p.324; CSP Domestic, p.31 Aug. 11, 1603; CSP James 1603-10 Jan. 4 & 19, 1604.

5 Bindoff, History of Parliament Vol. III & IV.

6 HMC XVI, p.445.

7 CSP Domestic, 1598-1601 p.426, and Boynton Lindsay, Studies in Political History, *The Elizabethan Militia 1558-1638*, p.43.

8 Later called, 'The Council for the Company of Adventurers and Planters in Virginia'; The Plymouth Company was the less successful company of the two and failed in 1620. It was then reorganised as the Council for New England.

9 *Genesis of the United States* Vols. 1 & 2.; HMC XIX, p.594 ; *Encyclopaedia Britannica* Vols. 7 & 9; Chambers *Biographical Dictionary*; The Virginia Company, and *The English Voyages of 16ᵗʰ Century* by Walter Raleigh published 1926, and Nicholl, *The Creature in the Map*.

10 Middlesex Sessions Rolls, June 20, 1608.

11 Remembrancia 1579-1664, p.246.

12 Registers of Westminster Abbey, p.183; Harleian. Soc. Vol. 10 and *Life of Thomas Bushell*, 1932.

13 Barratt Vol. I and Park, p.67/8.

14 Armagil 1568 – Grave No. CH97; Abigail – Grave No. XL028.

BOOKS

Sir William Waad supported the authors of many of the important manuscripts of his day like Lloyd's *State Worthies*, Rider's *Dictionary* (the first Latin dictionary to provide the Latin equivalent of English words as well as Latin into English), and Hooker's *Polity* amongst others. He owned many beautiful books, most of them now lodged at the Bodleian Library in Oxford. Waad also encouraged John Taylor, the Water Poet, who as a Thames waterman knew Waad well. In 1612 Taylor dedicated *The Sculler*, to 'The Right Worshipful and worthy favourer of learning, my singular good master, Sir William Waad, Knight'. Taylor had often collected the much disputed liquid wine duty for him from merchant ships passing up the river. In *Farewell to the Tower Bottles* in 1622, John Taylor wrote:

> "I was a waterman twice four long year
> And lived in a contented happy state
> Then turn'd the whirling wheel of fickle Fate
> From water unto wine: Sir William Waad
> Did freely and for nothing turn my trade,
> Ten years almost the place I did retain
> And glean'd great Bacchus' blood from France and Spain.
> But as men's thoughts a world of ways do range,
> So, as Lieutenants chang'd, did customs change."

We know from Lloyd's *State Worthies* that Rider's *Dictionary* was due to Sir William's 'directions', Hooker's *Polity* to his 'encouragement' and Gruter's *Inscriptions* to his 'charge'.

John Rider had produced a Latin dictionary in 1589 which was printed by Joseph Barnes, the printer to Oxford University. In his preface Rider acknowledges his debt to the Earl of Sussex and the right worshipful William Waad, Esquire, one of the Clerks of His Majesty's most honourable Privy Council. This dictionary is claimed to be the first Latin/English.

Waad had given considerable encouragement to Richard Hooker in his writing of that great work *The Laws of Ecclesiastical Polity*. The first four books were printed in 1593, the fifth volume in 1597 and the last three published posthumously in 1600. Hooker's work is wide-ranging and shows him to be one of the great religious thinkers of the period. His book came to be regarded as a sort of Bible of Precedent on which vital decisions by the Church of England were based. It was founded on scholarship but preached the middle way.

Inscriptionae Antiquai was produced by James Gruter in 1602. It is a vast collection of memorials, mainly from Roman times.

Waad's own books were left to his son, James, but some of them became the property of Archbishop Laud of Canterbury, the Chancellor of Oxford University, in 1633. Laud became a much-hated figure, who was violently anti-calvinist and was beheaded on Tower Hill by the Long Parliament in 1644 as 'guilty of endeavouring to overthrow the Protestant religion and act as an enemy to Parliament'. Some of these books had previously belonged to Armigel and nine of them remain in the Bodleian Library. One is a philosophical work translated from the Arabic into Latin by John Tripolitanneum. Another is a work on foreign languages, printed in Rome by Valerio Dorico in 1561 and a handwritten work in Latin. There is a copy of the *Gospels*, printed in London in 1571 and another Latin work given as a present to Lady Anne by Jacob Waad, as well as a superb illuminated book which is thought to have been printed by Caxton, dated on the flyleaf '1606 William Waad, Lieutenant of the Tower,' but this, too, had belonged to Armigel.

One wonderful work, signed by William in 1586, is a history book with many animals and saints in the margins, with three or four quarter and half-size pages of colourful pictures. There is also a book of coats-of-arms, hand-drawn, within printed heraldic outlines and a further volume written by hand, in French, about the death of Mary and the accession of Queen Elizabeth.

AN EXPLANATION OF THE BRITISH PEERAGE AND KNIGHTHOOD

The five British peerage ranks in order of seniority are duke, marquess, earl, viscount and baron.

Duke – the title of duke (from Latin Dux, a leader) was created by King Edward III in 1337 and is the most senior rank in the peerage. The wife of a duke is a duchess.

Marquess – the title of marquess (from the term Marchio), now ranks between duke and earl. The first 'marquess' was Robert de Vere, Earl of Oxford, when he was made Marquess of Dublin in 1385. The wife of a marquess is a marchioness.

Earl – the title of earl (derived from Scandinavian Jarl) is the oldest English title and rank. In the Middle Ages, it was placed below the rank of marquess. The wife of an earl is a countess. The continental equivalent of an earl is a count.

Viscount – the title of viscount (with its origins in Vice-Comes, a deputy or lieutenant of a Count) ranks between an earl and a baron. The wife of a viscount is a viscountess

Baron is the lowest rank of the peerage. It was introduced into England by the Norman kings. The first baron created by patent was by King Richard II in 1387. The wife of a baron is a baroness, addressed as 'Lady'.

Baronet is a hereditary dignity, however, **knight, esquire** and **gentleman** are *not* titles of nobility and do not form part of the peerage.

In Great Britain, a peer is **a noble**. The status of nobility does not extend to his wife or to his children. It is only when a peer dies that the eldest son inherits his father's title and becomes noble.

Lord: a man of noble rank or high office. A title given formally to a baron, and less formally to a marquess, earl or viscount (prefixed to a Christian name or territory), as in Lord Cobham, or Lord 'of the manor of...'

A **knight** was a warrior who served a nobleman or a nobleman who followed a king. Today a **knight** is a person who has been awarded a non-hereditary title by the sovereign and is entitled to use the honorific *Sir*. The wife of a knight is referred to as 'Lady...' The female non-hereditary title awarded by the sovereign is usually **Dame**.

DRAMATIS PERSONAE

JAMES I of England and VI of Scotland (1566-1625), son of Mary, Queen of Scots and Henry Stuart, Lord Darnley. James became King of England upon the death of Queen Elizabeth I in 1603. Married Anne of Denmark, daughter of King Frederick II of Denmark and sister of King Christian IV of Denmark.

SIR FRANCIS BACON (1561-1626), statesman and lawyer. Knighted in 1603 and made Solicitor General in 1607. Attorney General in 1616 and involved in the Overbury Trials. Lord Keeper in 1616-17 and Lord Chancellor 1618. Created Baron Verulam in 1618 and Viscount St. Albans in 1621. Found guilty of taking bribes and spent some time in the Tower.

GEORGE BROOKE (1568-1603), conspirator, youngest son of William Brooke, 10th Baron Cobham (1527-1597) and Frances Newton. He was involved in the Bye Plot and was executed in 1603. He was the brother of Henry, conspirator in the Main Plot.

HENRY BROOKE (died 1619), 11th **Lord Cobham**, conspirator, son of William Brooke, 10th Lord Cobham and Frances Newton. Henry was involved in the Main Plot and arrested but not executed. He was the brother of George Brooke, conspirator in the Bye Plot.

SIR HENRY BROOKE (1537-1592), (Cobham), diplomat, fifth surviving son of George Brooke, 9th Baron Cobham, (1487-1558), and Anne Bray. He was brother of William Brooke, 10th Baron Cobham (1527-1597). Henry used the family title of Cobham rather than the family name of Brooke. He succeeded Sir Amias Paulet as resident ambassador in France in October 1579. Friend of William Waad.

ROBERT CARR (c.1587-1645), Viscount Rochester, became **Earl of Somerset**, married Frances Howard who was divorced wife of Robert, 3rd Earl of Essex. Accused, with Frances, of being accessory to poisoning of Overbury.

ROBERT CECIL (1563-1612), Viscount Cranborne, then became **1st Earl of Salisbury** (1605). He was second son of William Cecil, (1st Baron Burghley). Became Principal Secretary of State in 1596 and held office till his death. Married Elizabeth Brooke, by whom he had a son William, and a daughter Frances.

WILLIAM CECIL (1520-1598), **1st Lord Burghley,** only son of Richard Cecil of Burleigh, Stamford, Northamptonshire and wife Jane Heckington. Married first to Mary Cheke, second wife Mildred, eldest daughter of Sir Anthony Cooke. Father of Thomas and Robert Cecil. In 1550 made Privy Councillor and one of secretaries of state. Became Lord High Treasurer in 1572.

SIR EDWARD COKE (1551-1633), judge and historian. Made Solicitor General in 1592 and Attorney General in 1594. Became Chief Justice of the Common Pleas in 1606, and Chief Justice of the King's Bench and Privy Councillor in 1613. Presided over the Overbury trials. Dismissed by the King in 1616 for 'perpetual turbulent carriage', and imprisoned in the Tower in 1622.

ROBERT DEVEREUX (1565-1601), 2nd **Earl of Essex**, soldier and politician. Eldest son of Water Devereux, 1st Earl of Essex (1539-1576). Became Ward of Court when his father died. Spent time as Cecil House and Theobalds, supervised by Lady Burghley, and mixed with Robert Cecil during his youth. Executed in 1601 for instigating the Essex Rebellion.

ROBERT DEVEREUX (1591-1646), 3rd **Earl of Essex**, son of 2nd Earl of Essex and Frances Walsingham. Married Frances Howard in 1606, divorced 1613.

SIR THOMAS EGERTON (1550? -1617), Solicitor General 1581, Attorney General 1592 and knighted 1593. Became Lord Chancellor in 1603 and given peerage **as Baron Ellesmere.**

FATHER HENRY GARNET (1555-1606), Head of the Jesuits in England. Accused of implication in the Gunpowder Plot and executed on May 3, 1606.

FATHER JOHN GERARD (1564-1637), Jesuit priest. Escaped from Tower of London in 1597, by rope across the moat.

FRANCES HOWARD (c.1593-1632), second daughter of Thomas Howard, Earl of Suffolk and his wife Katherine Knyvett. Married Robert Devereux and became Countess of Essex. Divorced him in 1613 and married Robert Carr to become Countess of Somerset. Tried for murder of Overbury.

HENRY III of France (1551-1589), King of France 1574-89. Suffered almost incessant civil war between Huguenots (Protestants) and Catholics led by Guise faction. Arranged assassination of the Duke of Guise.

HENRY IV of France (1553-1610), King of France 1589-1610. Previously Henry of Navarre. First Bourbon king of France.

HENRY HOWARD (1540-1614), second son of Sir Henry Howard, Earl of Surrey, (executed 1546/7). Younger brother of Thomas, 4th Duke of Norfolk (executed 1572), and uncle of Thomas, Earl of Suffolk. Became **Earl of Northampton** in 1604 and Lord Privy Seal in 1608. Brother-in-law to Sir Thomas Knyvett, keeper of the palace of Westminster, who found the barrels of gunpowder. Friend of Robert Carr.

THOMAS HOWARD (1561-1626), eldest son of Thomas, 4th Duke of Norfolk (executed 1572), by his second wife, Margaret Dudley, daughter and heir of Thomas Audley, Baron Audley of Walden. Created 1st **Earl of Suffolk** by King James I in 1603. Became Privy Councillor and Lord Chamberlain. Also Chancellor of Cambridge and Lord Treasurer. Considerably enlarged Audley End House, Saffron Walden, Essex. Buried in Saffron Walden church.

SIR HENRY MONTAGUE (1563-1642), judge and statesman. Recorder of London in 1603. Kings Serjeant-at-law, succeeded Sir Edward Coke as Chief Justice of the King's Bench in 1616. Opened the case against Somerset.

HENRY MORDAUNT (1568-1609), 4th Baron Mordaunt. From Drayton in Northamptonshire. Roman Catholic. Christina Keyes (wife of conspirator) was governess to Mordaunt's children.

SIR THOMAS OVERBURY (1581-1613), close friend of Robert Carr, (later Earl of Somerset) and member of court of King James I. Died at the Tower of London – believed poisoned.

NICHOLAS OWEN Born Oxfordshire and died in 1606 at the Tower of London. Called **"Little John"** because of his diminutive stature. Owen was the son of an Oxfordshire carpenter, and was himself a skilled builder and joiner prior to entering the Society of Jesus c. 1577. He constructed priest-holes to hide Jesuit priests from *'pursuivors'* (hunters of Catholics). Died at the Tower possibly under torture.

WILLIAM PARKER (1575-1622) **Lord Monteagle** (11th Baron Morley). Father, Edward Parker, 10th Baron Morley – recusant. His mother Elizabeth was the daughter and heiress of William Stanley, 3rd Lord Monteagle, and her mother was a firm supporter of the Jesuits. His younger brother Charles served with Ralegh in 1617, and sister Mary married Thomas Habington of Hindlip, Worcestershire. Through his mother he was connected to Thomas Howard, Earl of Arundel.

HENRY PERCY (1564-1632), 9th **Earl of Northumberland**, nobleman. Married Lady Dorothy Perrott, sister of Robert Devereux, 2nd Earl of Essex. Interested in science, medicine, anatomy and military matters. Incarcerated in the Tower on suspicion of involvement in the Gunpowder Plot. Released from the Tower in 1621.

THOMAS PERCY (1560-1605), Conspirator. Son of Edward Percy of Beverley. His grandfather, Josceline Percy (d.1532) was fourth son of Henry Percy, 4th Earl of Northumberland.

THOMAS PHELIPPES (c.1555-1625?), cryptographer and intelligence gatherer. Employed by Walsingham's intelligence service.

SIR JOHN POPHAM (c.1531-1607) Attorney-General, officiated at the trial of Mary Queen of Scots at Fotheringay. Knighted and became Lord Chief Justice in 1597. Presided over trials of Sir Walter Ralegh in 1603, and Guy Fawkes, in 1606. Lived at Littlecote Manor, near Chilton Foliat, Wiltshire from 1601.

SIR WALTER RALEGH (1552-1618), English courtier, navigator and poet, born in Hayes Barton, near Sidmouth Devon. Became favourite of Queen Elizabeth I. From 1584 to 1589 sent on expedition to America and despatched an abortive settlement to Roanoke Island, North Carolina (1585-6). Married Bessy Throckmorton. Implicated in the Main Plot in 1603 and committed to the Tower. Released in 1616 to find Eldorado, but during a failed expedition to the Orinoco he lost his son and his fleet. Beheaded at Whitehall in 1618.

LADY ARABELLA STUART (1575-1615), first cousin to King James I. Daughter of Charles Stuart, Earl of Lennox and his wife Elizabeth (née Cavendish). Grandaughter of Bess of Hardwick. Married William Seymour without the king's permission and was held under arrest until she died in the Tower.

WILLIAM SEYMOUR (1588-1660), 2nd Earl of Hertford and 3rd **Duke of Somerset**. Secretly married Lady Arabella Stuart, escaped custody and fled to France.

ANN VAUX (1562- ?), daughter of William Vaux and Elizabeth Beaumont, sister of Elizabeth Vaux. Never married. Friend of Father Garnet.

ELIZABETH VAUX (c.1560-1625), daughter of William Vaux and Elizabeth Beaumont. Married Edward Brooksby (1577).

ARMIGEL WAAD (c.1511-1568), diplomat and adventurer. Born in Yorkshire, educated Magdalen College, Oxford, voyaged to North America in 1536. Became Clerk of Council of Calais in 1540, and

Clerk of the Privy Council 1547. Married first Anne Marbury, second Alice Patten. Sons William and Thomas.

SIR FRANCES WALSINGHAM (1530-1590), appointed one of the principal secretaries of State to Queen Elizabeth I, and shared administrative responsibilities of government with Lord Treasurer Burghley. Sworn onto Privy Council and knighted. Created a highly successful system of espionage at home and abroad.

PRINCIPAL CONSPIRATORS IN THE GUNPOWDER PLOT:

Robert Catesby
John (Jack) Wright
Thomas Wintour
Guy Fawkes
Thomas Percy
Robert Keyes
Thomas Bates
Christopher (Kit) Wright
Robert Wintour
John Grant
Ambrose Rookwood
Francis Tresham
Sir Everard Digby

ACKNOWLEDGEMENTS

GRATEFUL THANKS TO THE following institutions for their kindness and tolerance with all the wheelchair problems during our research.

British Library
Bodleian Library, Oxford
Cambridge University Library
National Archives (PRO)
Cambridge Record Office
Camden Local Studies
Essex Record Office
Hertfordshire Record Office
Middlesex Record Office
Saffron Walden Library, Local Studies Department

BIBLIOGRAPHY

Primary Sources:
Manuscripts:
Birch MS 4109, f.343
Lansdown MS 153
MS Rawlinson D.1160 & D.183 (Bodleian)
MS Laud misc. 132, 316, 471, 479, 565, 589, 660, 708 (Bodleian)
Gunpowder Plot Book (PRO, SP14/216 – all)
PRO PROB 11/46 Will of Sir Humphrey Browne
PRO PROB 11/52 Will of Armigel Waad
PRO PROB 11/ Will of Owen Waller
ERO T/A 714 Prob. 11/142 Will of Sir William Waad : PCC 6 Lyon
ERO D/P 272/1 & 2, Manuden Church Registers,
ERO T/P 195/15, William Holman Manuscript History of Essex
ERO D/CR 237, Bishops' Transcripts
Probate of Thomas Wade Reg. 86 Dixy
Acts of the Privy Council, editors J.R. Dasent and others, 1890- 1964. 1615, 1616
Calendar & Index of Patent Rolls, 31-37 Elizabeth
Calendar of Patent Rolls, 17-30 Elizabeth
Calendar of State Papers Domestic Elizabeth 1581-90
Calendar of State Papers Domestic Elizabeth 1598-1601
Calendar of State Papers Foreign Elizabeth 1562 and 1571-3
Calendar of State Papers Domestic James I, 1603-10
Calendar of State Papers Spanish 1587
Calendar of State Papers Venetian, 1579, and 1587
Essex Feet of Fines, 1423-1547, Vol. 4

Essex Feet of Fines, 1547-1580, Vol. 5

Essex Feet of Fines, 1581-1603, Vol. 6

Foster Pedigrees of Yorkshire Families, Vol. 2 York & W. Riding and Vol. 3 North East Riding.

Foedera VI Pt. IV 1565 (Patents)

HMC Cecil Vol. V (The Hatfield Papers)

HMC Salisbury Papers Part XXIII Addenda 1562 – 1605 HMSO 1973 540.02.c.2.23a

HMC Salisbury Papers Pt XIV

HMC Salisbury Papers Pt XVII, 1938

HMC Salisbury XVIII, 1940

HMC Salisbury XIX

HMC Earl of Marr & Kellie

HMC Marquess of Downshire Vol. 4

Bishop of London Registers

London Marriage Licenses

Register of Admission to Gray's Inn, 1521-1889

Registers of the Privy Council

Registers of Westminster Abbey – ed. Col. J.L. Chester

Richard Symonds Manuscript 1639 (Collectanea) Vols. II and III

Mort Commons

Harleian Soc. Vol. 10

Primary Source Books:

Barratt, Thomas J. *The Annals of Hampstead,* 1912

Biddle, Richard, *A Memoir of Sebastian Cabot,* 1831

Bindoff, S., History of Parliament Vol. III & IV. 1982

Dixon,William Hepworth, *Her Majesty's Tower,* 1870, Vols I and II

Dictionary of National Biography, OUP, 2004 (online version) and older version DNB Vol.50

Edwards, Francis, *Guy Fawkes, The Real Story of the Gunpowder Plot?* 1969

Foster, J. Alumni Oxoniensis 1500-1714, Oxford, 1892

Foxe's Book of Martyrs, (1865 version – Rev. J. Milner), London

Froude, James, Anthony, *History of England,* Vol. III, XII & XI, 1870

Fuller, Dr., *Worthies of Yorkshire*, 1868-76

Gruter Janus, *Inscriptiones antiquae Romani*, 1602

Haklyt, *Divers Voyages Touching the Discovrie of America*, 1582

Hening, *Genesis of the United States*, Vols. 1 & 2, 1890

Hooker, R., *Laws of Ecclesiastical Polity*, 1554-1603

Geare J.G., *Farnham, Essex Past and Present*, 1858

Gerard, John, *The Autobiography of an Elizabethan*, (Trans. Philip Caraman) 1951

Goodman, Dr. Godfrey, *The Court of James I*, 1839

Jardine, David, *Narrative of the Gunpowder Plot*, 1857

Lloyd, David, *'State Worthies'*, 1766

Morant, Philip, *TheHistory & Antiquities of The Count of Essex*, Vol. II, c. 1768 reprints 1816, 1978.

Morris, J., (ed.), *Amias Paulet letter books*, 1874

Nichols, John, *Progresses of King James I*, Vol. I, 1838

Park, J.J., *The Topography & Natural History of Hampstead*, 1850

Rymer, Thomas, (ed.), *Foedera*, The Hague, 1739

Sawyer, Edmund, *Papers of Sir Ralph Winwood*, 1725

Tesimond, Oswald, *The narrative of Oswald Tesimond alias Greenway*, (translation by Francis Edwards of the Stonyhurst Manuscript), 1973

Remembrancia 1579-1664

Rider, John, *Bibliotheca Scholastica*, Oxford 1589

Stowe, *Survey of Cities of London & Westminster*, 1663 edition, 1720

Taylor, John, *The Water Poet, Collected Works*, 1612

Wade, Charles, Stuart, *The Wade Genealogy*, NY 1900

Weldon, Anthony, *Court and Character of James I*, 1811

Bushell, *The Life of Thomas Bushell*, 1932

Secondary Sources – Books:

Akrigg, G.P.V. (Ed), *Letters of King James VI & I*, University of California, 1984

Boynton, Lindsay, *Studies in Political History*, 'The Elizabethan Militia' 1558-1638, 1982

Caraman, Philip, *Henry Garnet 1555-1606, and the Gunpowder Plot*, 1964

Carswell, Donald., *Trial of Guy Fawkes*, Notable British Trials Series, 1934

Chancellor, E. Beresford, *Annals of the Strand*, 1919

Beckingsale, B.W., *Burghley, Tudor Statesman 1520-1598*, 1967

Bevan, Bryan, *King James VI of Scotland & 1 of England*, 1996

Du Maurier, Daphne, *The Golden Lads*, 1975

Durant, David N., *Arabella Stuart: a rival to the Queen*, 1978

Fraser, Antonia, *The Gunpowder Plot, Terror & Faith in 1605*, 1996

Handover, P.M., *The Second Cecil, The Rise to Power 1563-1604 of Sir Robert Cecil, later first Earl of Salisbury*, 1959

Hurst, Michael, *Studies in Political History*, 'The Elizabethan Militia'

Lacy, Robert, *Sir Walter Raleigh*, 1973

Lindley, David, *The Trials of Frances Howard*, 1993

Morgan, George, Blacker, *The Great English Treason*, 1931

McGurk, John, *The Tudor Monarchies 1485-1603*, CUP 1999

McInnes, Ian, *Arabella – The Life & Times of Lady A. Seymour*, 1957

Murray, John, *Cast of Ravens*, 1965

Nicholls, Mark, *Investigating Gunpowder Plot*, Manchester University Press, 1991

Northcote Parkinson, C., *Gunpowder Treason and Plot*, 1976

Plowden, Alison, *Danger to Elizabeth*, 1974

Rosser, Gervase, *Medieval Westminster 1200-1540*, 1989

Seel & Smith, *Crown & Parliaments 1558-1689*, CUP, 2001

Somerset, Anne, *Unnatural Murder*, 1997

Stowe, John, *A Survey of London* (reprinted from text of 1603), Vol I & II, OUP, 1971

Venn, J, *Alumni Cantabrigienses*, Cambridge, 1924

Winchester, Barbara, *Tudor Family Portrait*, 1955

Serials:

Barnett, Richard, C., 'Place, Profit and Power', *James Sprunt Studies in History and Political Science, Vol 51*, University of North Carolina Press, 1969

Harris, P.R. (ed.), 'The Reports of William Udall, Informer, 1606-

16120, *Recusant History,* VIII nos. 4 & 5, pp 192-184.

Sprott, S.E., 'Sir Edmund Baynham', Recusant *History,* X, pp 96-110

Wake, Joan, 'The Death of Francis Tresham', *Northamptonshire Past and Present,* 2, 1954

INDEX

138

139

About the Author

Born in Lancashire, the author lived and worked in France, and in the USA, before returning to settle on the Essex/Hertfordshire border during the 1970s. A first degree in Humanities from the Open University led to further pursuit of her interest in history in the form of a Cambridge University Masters' degree in history. Fiona has been involved in history in the community for over 20 years, and has written articles in academic journals as well as producing a number of booklets on subjects of local interest.

Printed in the United Kingdom by
Lightning Source UK Ltd., Milton Keynes
140306UK00001B/120/A

9 781412 055413